MADE FROM MIDNIGHT

A Poets in the Pines Anthology

curated & edited by

KELLY MILLER

ANNE RAMALLO

LEAH CASS

illustrated by

EMILY DANIEL

ISBN: 978-1-960143-11-2

poetsinthepines.com

TABLE OF CONTENTS

EDITORS' NOTE

This collection takes an unflinching look at death and grief. As in life, people die in the following pages—of age, illness, suicide, and acts of violence. Wave after wave, movement after movement, death keeps coming. This book is not intended to be read in one sitting, so please take breaks, cry, release, and remember: we do not aim to fill the holes left in you, because it's not possible. Still, we hope this collection helps you to process, frame, and find meaning in these events, as our writers have done through their words.

Please take care of yourselves on this journey through the long night. Even here, in the dark, we have charted for you a map of stars.

This book is dedicated to our contributors, who shared their ghosts, offered up their voices, and sat in the darkness with us.

Thank you.

PRELUDE

The Light Shifts

DELUGE

CHRISTIAN CHASE GARNER

A bass boat sputters
into the bosom
of the forlorn
lake water—brown,
like roasted bone
marrow. The captain
lets his son
rest in a small,
makeshift
tackle box, a
tomb, watching
the storm clouds
swell.
He waits.
A snap
of lightning
threads
the sky.

PART ONE

A Pulled-Out Tooth

WHEN YOU REACH THE FRONT OF THE LINE

CAROL DORF

Last night I called your name to remind you
to breathe. When the widows post status updates

I contemplate your mortality, not mine,
though I warned our offspring they would need

to step up for you if I went first. Where do
you go? None of my dead have answered

that question clearly. Like the cat pawing for
attention after I return from an absence,

I would like to be explicit. Would it
have helped if Chana had titled her last book,

Dying for Dummies? The mail truck is outside
but news never comes in the post—instead

there's an email or a call too early
in the morning. Sometimes I watch moths flutter

through the yard on another dry day. Today
I woke to the crows' raucous complaints.

WEARY

LAUREN MADSEN

Stars still shine outside the window when she pulls off
the covers and walks quietly across the floor,
her fingertips grazing the top of their wedding portrait as she goes,
the next hour to herself necessary, yet costly.

Soon he will wake, and she will be ready to help him
sit up and slowly shuffle to the bathroom.
Tired arms lowering him onto and lifting him off of the toilet
loving hands washing his wrinkled body in the shower.
She will take a deep breath before struggling to pull
on his shirt and pants, his uncontrolled movements reminding her
of dressing their wiggly toddlers another lifetime ago.
The coming hours will look much the same—
labored trips to the bathroom from the couch and back again
'til it's time to ready him for bed, and a rest for them both.

Finishing her toast and swallowing the last of her milk,
she whispers another prayer for this, another day,
as she wonders how many more like it
she has left.

MARMALADE ORANGE

BILLY EASTON

Marmalade orange heartbreak
in the middle of a road.

Not knowing, a girl
by a window
anticipates her playmate.
Grasps a ball of yarn, rolls
it out. Imagines fat
paws batting it away,
chasing it. Giggles.

She waits.
Her emotional marrow
not yet shredded.

She doesn't know
that
golden eyes,
once sparkling,
now stare
unmoving nothingness
at the world.

Agony lurks,
back arched,
waiting to pounce,

claws sharper
than any cat.

FLEETING LIGHT

ELI ROOKE

my love
teach me how to die quietly
in the night without a fuss
let me slip away without inconvenience or burden
I want to learn how to leave so you won't mourn me

I take it back my love
teach me how to die loudly
roaring thrashing and bringing the sky down with me
I want to be ripped away and leave you
a wound you can never heal from

my love please
teach me how to die with dignity
I have spent my whole life trying to be a man
and do not want to lose it when the pain comes
don't let me howl and beg and sob
let me die without being unsightly

my love speak softly
teach me that it is inevitable
death comes for everyone but my soul is sprinting
and I am begging to stop tell me it's okay to stop
lie so I can try and believe you

my liar I'm a liar
please don't teach me to die bravely
let me whisper I'm scared but dig my heels in

let my hands tremble as they hold the
fraying edges of the cosmos together
let me scream as it hurts let me cry when I realize
my love isn't enough to keep you

let me beg the universe to survive this
let me come back to you
let me come back
let me

my love
before I die teach me how to live
I have spent so long waiting for the end
I have forgotten how to breathe
hold me please
let dying come tomorrow

DARLING, PUT ON THE STRING OF PEARLS

JOSH STONE

Battle cry growing louder
tiny figurines crest the hill, turning into giants
marching with guns and guillotines

my only armor, this single picked flower
let me place it on your ear
behind the curl
darling, put on the string of pearls
I can hold them back no longer
it's time to fight

the mob shouts my name
no rest until there's blood
I will not sacrifice this lovely life
No!
I will not betray our sons

take this weapon,
velvet black and silken gold
that dress I bought
last summer
will you wear it now?
it's time to fight

your brown eyes
my god

all of the bullets
none of the gun
hold my hand
kiss my cheek
we will take them one by one

it's midnight darling
the hour has come
shall we dance in this
firefight
potter's field

THE WAITING ROOM

KEEGAN GORMALLY

I was told you would leave,
but not how.
Not whether it would happen
in the corner of a room
or a crease between days.

I keep imagining the way the body
thinks it can hide something:
a bruise,
a cough,
the slow collapse of the lungs
as if they were saving up
for something they would never speak aloud.

Yet you said those two words
once—*I'm dying*
the words you did not speak twice—
but you found solace in them

as if they were in a cup
you offered me,
and you could hold it
just long enough
to forget it was burning you.

The light shifts
I watch a bird outside your window for hours
but the window stays shut.

There is nothing to hear
but the space between breaths,
a sound
you can only understand
when it fades, when it's gone.

They said you would fade, too,
"slowly, then all at once"
several of the nurses said,
a cliché used so often there
it never needs the dust blown off it.

Then you died to the sound
of Debussy's "Prelude to the Afternoon of a Faun."

Death, you once told me,
is a failed rehearsal:
everyone dressed up around you,
the lights adjusted,
but no one enters on cue.

POEM IN WHICH WE ARE TWO BUTTERFLIES SPINNING IN A CIRCLE OVER THE HIGHWAY

J.N.V

I never saw the car.
Only you.

> *Always you.*

SHE REACHES DOWN WAY—
SEEKING PAST MEMORY'S LOCK

ABBY LUBY

her lover's tether fades as he leaves the earth fingers still tapping
notes on his violin, singing

      curly vines   wa-wa vibrato   spilling filling

 inner lush-plucks like flutters—fish gills' last gasp.

His slack hand in hers, the waning off-beat pulse
like a stutter stuck on a syllable. Then, under blinking fluorescents

      blue-gloved nurse banishes his ashen limp hands
into crusty, sanitized paper mittens
      crack slap rip of Velcro, his sweet palms stolen.

Stops   med-tube yank-out & face scratching   says doc,
merciless & bolting from medical industrial sprawl, and here
      are futile heart pumps

She steps back as his trapped bony tendrils
flexed through decades of caresses, of tickling a warm baby's nose
      fingers   that deftly cracked eggs with one hand
charming her for 60 years.

DANGEROUS TASTE

ÖZGE LENA

That winter evening
far forests were burning,
and tanker planes needling
the bleeding sphere.
A wind was bringing us
the dangerous taste of death
while lying on an overturned
boat in the dry lake, your arm
on my shoulder, proud collar
of my life, soft and precious.
After a moment of sour silence
to watch the approaching disaster,
you told me that the death of someone
you love must be like a pulled-out tooth,
sore at first with a lush blood clot, aching
unbearably as the tongue pokes and pokes
the cavity. Soon the wound closes, the mouth
gets used to the emptiness, the tongue calms
down at the place where once was a deep pain.
Then you kissed my tongue, slow and delicious.
Three evenings later when you were gone,
it was like I had all my teeth pulled out, all my life
was uprooted, my tongue—a whirligig in my mouth.

GRIEF WITHIN A DREAM

MARY M. BROWN

is a hunger, a hammer, a hound
    that pursues you, restless nights,
a mountain of ice and you without

a pick, a coat, a prayer, you
    without the means to build a fire,
without a match, a bridge, a rearview

mirror, with only a missing button,
    broken latch, invisible handle,
great big hook without an eye

IF I STOP

MARK HERNANDEZ

—for Grandma Sandra

With each whisk, the batter circles around the bowl.
It reminds me of the steady pace I had to keep
as I tried to revive you. The constant movement
around the bowl—I can't over-beat
the eggs. I was told to slow the rhythm. Over-
beating would make me start over. I can't.
If I stop, the dough will flatten.
If I stop, you won't catch your breath. I must
fold in the egg whites gently.

JUST FOR NOW

LAYNIE TZENA

Try not to talk
about loss. People
decide you are

canvas, they are
paint, or, say,
you have a new life

as a recording device, or
they take you as their own
glass to fill with sorrow,

you just overflow. So you
practice saying, "Fine," and
sometimes it's even true.

You want to say, "Look,
right here, right now
I can actually think,

and no, I don't
want to hear about
someone you know
who died, too.
I want you to
leave me alone,

not leave me alone,
what I mean is
let me tell you

when it's time
to talk about it,
just for now."

ARBORIST FOR THE BLUES

DEZ NAPOLEON

Didn't want a headstone.
Didn't want a place for people
to lay flowers
and lie about how they showed up
when you were breathing.

I wanted a fight.
I wanted something to rip up the ground,
like you ripped through life—
loud, laughing, cussing, loving.

So I dug a hole.
Shoved a tree down into it.
Told the dirt:
Hold him like I couldn't.
Grow him bigger than grief.

And if that tree leans ugly,
if it splits in storms,
if it throws down rotten fruit—
good.
It's honest.
It's real.
It's you.

DREAM IN WHICH YOU DID NOT DIE

KAYLA SARGESON

You:

        on a picnic bench
        wearing a blue flannel shirt
        dark jeans
        your gross moccasins
        legs crossed

laughing
mouth open

I reach out—

and for a couple lovely seconds

I forget—

wake up right as my hand almost touches your face

MY FATHER IN THE DAYS BEFORE HIS DEATH

JEANNE WAGNER

was like a bird flapping against a window

because he had a head as small as
a pecan shell, light as a blown egg,

a hard stiletto beak, long, slender
bones as hollow as a bird's feet.

His own feet curled into commas,
his wings wide as cabbage leaves,

as reckless as the wind. At night
he longed to nestle in the eaves,

part bat and moth as well as bird.
He made wild fluttering sounds

like a wound in a bellows, a wind
guttering an open flame.

He struck at windowpanes, glanced
off the linoleum. He was a tracer

bullet, an ack-ack gun. Once he flew
so low, he threaded the table legs,

then swooped back up onto center
stage, and oh, I'm ashamed to say

I wanted to clap my hands and shoo
him away, open the windows wide,

make flapping motions with my wrists
until he flew outside, free again,

to lose himself in the oblivious air,
as vast and seamless as the night.

PRELUDE

MARK HERNANDEZ

I could use a thunderstorm right now.
The fog is too loud.
Dawn breaks

behind the haze,
but I still wait to feel
the warm sun. I can't

see what lies ahead.

The salt and the sea disorient me.
The wailing waves provide
no comfort. Crashes of wind
and water resonate profoundly.

I stay drunk
so reality can't
destroy me.

Confession lurks
beneath active waters.

I stay submerged unlike
Aphrodite. I can't
wash my hands clean
in the abyss found
between two
worlds. The sun won't
stand still for me. Celestial oceans
don't exist.

And I never learned
how to grieve.

WAKE

STELLA STOCKER

My sister is alive and I see her dead on bad nights,
in the dreams of people I love and haven't met reaching
for each other in the dark. She is there,

pinkish and floating. So unlike her
to be aimless, let alone wandering through my
silver sleep.

I lay on the couch as a horror movie plays, wondering
if my family is happy, if I am, and what is
happiness anyway.

I get angry at the jump-scare ghosts and sad when
they moan sweet nothings to the empty rooms
and fruit bowls, each apple a milky flesh eardrum.

My mom loves graveyards. She feels safe, alone
except for the smoke shapes of people and
tendrils of fondness etched in the stones. There, the dead
are marked and you know who is under your feet

because the names tell,
saying why they matter in the same letters.

OLD FAMILY MAGIC

MARY M. BROWN

He taught you
to disappear
when you
were with him,
schooled you

in the safety
of silence
since your voice
set him off,
sent him

back to some
earlier time,
to Viet Nam
or an even earlier
war,

the service he
had enlisted in
long before
you became his
bomb

Now that he
is gone, you
are in shock
at how real
your grief

is, how
explosive
your pain You
discover it on
your face

in the mirror
when you
finally see
yourself
reappear

ILLS AND INK SPILLS

KATE DAVIS

—for Leonard

I picked up a
last piece of you
procured mindlessly:
a pen in the pocket
of a bag I had found.

Like you, it can't be erased
staining a bruise on my palm
with each calendar reminder
in black ink that can't be replaced.

The weight is haunting,
a pocket's pressure,
though it's no burden that I carry.
Only a pen; my soul
bared for anyone to see.

I'll take my own advice
and treat it as any other.
To save it would condemn it—
much worse to go unused.

One odd day it was gone
somewhere it won't be found.
Though through this loss
an ending was avoided:
the ink never did run dry.

Gone, and in its place
the feeling of your unfinished story
in the green light
of the banker's lamp:
notes of days you should've seen.

BLACK DIAMOND

ANNE RAMALLO

You grew a 60-pound watermelon last summer
and cut it open a still-green cucumber—
picked too early.
"Next spring," you say from your jumble of wires—
"next spring we'll go up to Yuba City and get some of those…
What do you call them, Pat?
Black Diamond seeds."

No one contradicts you.
We don't want to cut the yarn you're spinning.
Here we are, a stalemate.
These wires, this oxygen
fragile filaments tying you to us.
You were always hard to tie down.

Black Diamond.
I cling to that, turn it over,
mining each facet for a metaphor.
Black Diamond. I'm desperate
for this to be beautiful.
But the light gets lost. Absorbed.

In the end, it will be like your last watermelon
waiting on the counter at home.
We cut it open: a piece of you,
over-ripe, tasting of earth and sun.
We eat it, savor it,
wish it sweeter, but in the end
it will be a pile of seeds—
wet, shining gems.
And we'll throw them away.
You were the one who planted seeds.

Unable to coax life, I cut
and I polish. Over and over
(another spin, another spin)
looking for a sparkle.

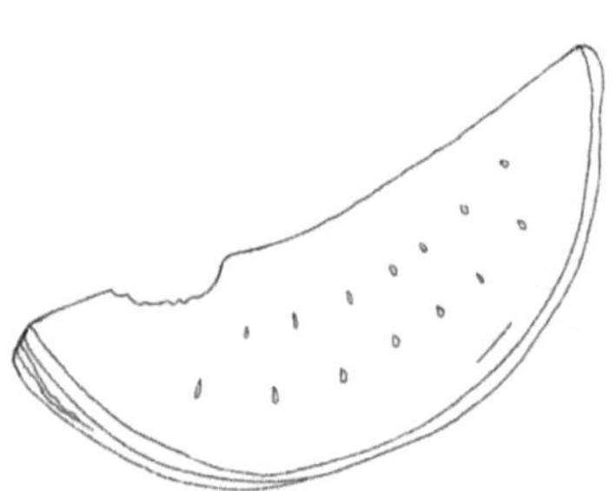

A FISHING POEM

NATHAN LESLIE

At five I snagged a three-pound bass
on a miscast into the reeds.
But that was my peak.
On a boat in the Severn we caught
eels, crabs, bluegills, croakers.
My uncle bashed a hooked bluegill
with the stub of an oar.
I had to look away.
The crabs clawed at the kitchen pot
as the water bubbled to a boil.

Poets craft gauzy lines:
fly fishing in the Missouri,
paddling out to a rock
in Lake Superior,
bobbers dancing in eddies,
worms dangling in crystal waters,
the men silent, stoic—a salty, mythic bond.

My young cousin reads her biology
book. She cocks her head, asks me:
"What does vestigial mean?"
I grab a bag from the freezer,
nod us to the creek.
We walk down the mossy stairs,
to the dock, the air ripe
with tar and moldering wood.

The creek is gray with effluence,
and fish float belly up
bobbing on the rainbow crests
of motorboats. I open the bag,
grasp the heads and tails,
the eyeballs and crimson guts,
toss the chum into the creek,
and then I point. Blood sputum:
all this in the end.

BUT THIS WAS BEFORE THE RAIN

J.M. SUMMERS

But this was before the rain.
Gathered on the doorstep,
rolled cigarettes, fumbled hands,
a cold inside and out.
Observing the iced hillside,
the comings, the goings?
Too busy either to register
laden skies, the whisper that
bears word of an oncoming storm.
What profit is there to be found here?
From the trees the rise of
squabbling crows, wings mimicking
the indifference of
bloody, fallen rain.

THE TRAIN RUMBLES BY

RUSSELL REECE

Bud, my cat, crouches at the edge of the dock, watches leaves, pine needles, goose feathers, small branches float past. He's engrossed with the stream of debris when a child-sized doll floats toward him, face up, arms spread. He looks at me, wide eyed, as if he wants to be sure I see it too. The doll hits the piling and turns around facing us, momentarily pinned by the moving tide. The body is covered in gray fabric and marsh slime; long auburn hair undulates around a muddy head and I think it's not a doll at all—it's a child; and I'm back along the railroad tracks, heart pounding, train thundering past as I wipe cinders from bloody scrapes on my hands and arm.

Another lost soul
another set of vacant eyes
staring up at me.

A WAR POEM

RONNA MAGY

—after Gertrude Stein

In history the present revives the past the past repeats
the present again once the mind conceives of killing and death
once the mind looks down the barrel of a gun gas and guns
take over the mind and in mind's eye will be nothing but death
nothing different the forest the trees the forest the trees
the unmarked graves when you hide in war's forests there are
no trees where can you walk where there are no graves once
the trees are cut down what happens to breath

HALF TRUTHS

LORI HETTEEN

Go on and try to describe a wake
of vultures dressed in mourning robes

without the mention of death. There is no
skirting the issue of why they're gathered

today in the sight of God and everyone.
A full grave of grisly facts includes rot.

Likewise, dear heart, when surveying
a pile of bones picked and licked clean

washed and weathered by the sun,
one can surmise somewhere up in the blue

is a cloud of witnesses who has
taught pounds of flesh to fly.

WAITING BY THE WINDOW

ELIZA CASS

Age 7

Now that you are home, I run to the kitchen. I was watching for you out the window. How was work? What did you do? I say everything but "I missed you and I jump for joy when I see you pull into the driveway." That's not what we say. I watch you heat up your dinner. Sometimes I am not allowed in the kitchen but you tell me I can stay. I am delighted. You look tired. I try not to talk to you too much. If you don't notice me, I can stay with you longer. You tell me I need to do better in school and I start to cry. Do you love me? You never say you love me. You start to speak and I think you're going to send me to bed. Instead you say, "Do you want my brownie?" You don't say I love you. That's not what we say.

Age 17

Now that you are home, I run to my bedroom. I was watching for you out the window. I didn't go to work and you are going to be very angry. "What is that smell?" "You're not to see that boy anymore." I would give anything not to be interrogated in this kitchen. I don't want to watch you eat dinner. You're disappointed in me and I am mad at you. You tell me I need to focus on school. I roll my eyes, I don't cry anymore. You start to speak and I think you're going to yell. Instead you say theres a movie on AMC, would I like to watch it? Its very good, I'll love it. Later that night I had to call you to pick me up from the police station. You don't say I love you. That's not what we say.

Age 29

Now that you are home, my daughter runs to see you. She was watching for you out the window. You work less and smile more. "What is that smell?" "We made you cookies." When did I become Betty Crocker? I need to be nicer to that boy. We all sit down to dinner. My daughter sits on your lap and you sneak her soda. I pretend not to see. That's not what we do. You start to speak and I know what you're about to say. "Pap Pap's girl is the smartest girl in school," directed towards her, but winking at me. At night you read stories and give hugs. You double check the doors and awake at the drop of a pin. You check on every room to ensure safety. I pretend to be asleep. You don't say I love you. That's not what we say.

Age 33

Now that you are gone, I run to your grave. I still think I see you out of every window. Memories of you are sometimes vivid and sometimes faint. I work too much. I don't talk to that boy anymore. Pap Pap's girl is doing fine, she talks about you all the time. I give her my brownies. She could do better in school. At night I read stories and double check the doors. I peek her in rooms and make sure everyone is okay. I say I love you. That's what we say.

STILL

R.M. DAVENPORT

He was still
in a pressed suit,
with little pinstripes and
a white boutonniere, like he might
sit up and say he was very, very late.

No one
says how late he
really had been when he
was all tubes in untrimmed nostrils,
and tanks of explosive gas on wheels.

He was still
in a pressed suit,
and he looked nothing
like the tremendous smile and
echoing laugh I had known all my life.

I stood beside
the velvet-lined box,
and slip in a paper I had wrote
in my sprawling handwriting in magic
marker and broken crayons. We were still.

SITTING ON TOP OF MY FATHER'S BONES WHILE STRANGE MEN EXPLAIN THINGS TO ME IN MY COMMENTS

LEAH CASS

I ask him what to do
Feet sinking into the earth
While fire lights my belly
Strange men tell me I don't understand

I take a drive with his ghost
He tells me there is more for me
But I can't hear where to find it
Strange men tell me to answer them

I catch my wraith staring
In the rearview mirror
Grandmothers in Adirondack chairs
Strange men tell me I should know my place as a woman

GRANITE AND BONE

DANIEL GONZALEZ

On the days I'm brave to walk across the evergreen lawn
To stare at your grave, daydream, and ramble on
As if you were still here to indulge me
Your bones may be near, just below me
But you aren't really there, are you?

Still, I feel you. Radiate from the afterlife. Or from heaven. purgatory? hell? Whatever you call the place in the ground where you rest. Is it really even a place? I wish you could answer me. And tell me if you're having fun. Anything to ensure me that you understand, I tried everything to keep you alive.

I avoid stepping where I think your body lays, to decorate your grave for your favorite holiday. My abuela used to say it was bad luck and a sin to step on a grave. And my guilt amplifies with you in every way. The statues of saints and depressed angels stare at me with everlasting haste, to say my peace and be gone, and let you rest in that place. All I ask is, can you hear me? Or am I talking to myself again.

The wind gathers at your grave when I whisper your name into the breeze, or is that you rattling the last of the barren trees leaves? Every butterfly that passes me by is your soul reincarnated. It's impossible yet true, I wholly know it's you. Coincidence leaves nothing to the imagination. No faith in reality, no hope for god. But one thing is certain: Both granite and bone fall to the earth and rot.

I want to claw at the dirt, ignore the pain as my nails bleed, and find you warm and tangible as I do in memories. Have you witnessed my new hobby? Putting picture frames up of all our moments. Just so you can occupy each corner of my empty dwelling.

54

> I don't see you in dreams because I hardly sleep.
> Not with your final moments haunting over me.
> But on this side of Earth, I like to think I visit you often
> To appease our souls and make sure you are never forgotten.

TO BE PLAYED ON FLUTE

ALESA BERNAT

—after W. B. Yeats "A Prayer for Old Age"

You were built to be played on flute—
though a flute is no longer
made of bone.
I imagine you as a fugue—
if ever a flute played a fugue.
A fugue as a form in poetry—
where lips and tongue
and teeth claim more body.

A song where your bones whistle—
a sorrowful tune, pitch-bending,
mumbling a dark timbre.

PART TWO

The Unspooling

I ONCE BELIEVED

JOANNE HARRIS ALLRED

that descending into death's grotto, you'd hear
the drip of a spring hidden deeper,
like the plink of piano keys

playing a tune you had forgotten
you loved. A shimmer off mossy walls

would brighten the emptying skull,
warming the cave where your past shivers.
Answers would bloom to questions

that had brought you to your knees or
dragged you behind horses of despair and desire

and your life would suddenly add up,
even suffering purposeful and holy,
transmuted to knowing,

and at last you'd see the whole picture.

As if there *were* a whole picture, and the game
is to wander sightless through its maze,

so when the blindfold is stripped
you can laugh, finally in on the joke, at all the dead
ends and wrong turns you crawled through like a beggar.

While, from the shadows, Time
chuckled to the Soul, coughing into a silk handkerchief,
impeccably dressed heartless killer that it is.

THIRTEEN WAYS OF LOOKING AT DEATH

ALISON STONE

Family gathered round. Morphine drip. Death.
Shown by the heart monitor's last blip—death.

I tell my kid "Holy Ghost" is a bad
translation. It sounds like they worship death!

No ceremony keeps them here. Despite
a choir or Oscar Wilde quip, death

has the last word at every funeral.
Paint on makeup, close the casket, zip death

into a bag—no matter. Gone is gone.
Did greed or boredom make the wife slip death

into her husband's drink? The sly moon's seen
everything. In bars, broken men sip death.

The aim of learning to build a fire—
survival. The goal of marksmanship—death.

Thetis dunked her son in the River Styx,
only one heel kept out of the dip. Death

be not proud. John Donne claimed God will wake us.
What pirates leave on the victims' ship—death.

Dionysius was born from Zeus' thigh.
The Fates hold our threads, ready to snip. Death's

depicted as both fiend and seducer.
We long to slay the demon or rip death

from a loved one's arms. Some suicides dress
in good suits or fur. Others strip for death.

Stone's fine with birth, youth, middle and even
(healthy) old age. Why can't we just skip death?

RECALL, RECALL, RECALL

RANDAL ELDON GREENE

Recall the Christmas party? Just days before she died. My niece, recently turned two, a miniature image of her mother. Grandparents in the rockers. Cousins climbing the couch. Wrapping paper flying about. New toys rolling, rumbling, whistling around. My sister fussing over her only daughter, my niece. Blond curls, blue eyes. No sign of a flu. No warning of the fluid-filled lungs to come. No sign of anything.

Recall her eyes, wide with curious wonder? Legs of the other children running by. Adults laughing, sipping hot cider. Christmas music crooning from the stereo. No hint of a fever. No knowing that IV fluid would let her linger with us in a tiny hospital crib. No idea that this would be her final Christmas.

Recall how she loved the Christmas tree? Green and synthetic. I can only imagine how it looked, that angel-topped conifer with those little colored lights. Blue and red and yellow and pink and green. How tempting for her, those bright, glowing dots of joy. She kept reaching out for them, and we kept telling her no. We stopped her hands and we told her no. We told her no. No.

DEATHLESS

ÖZGE LENA

They believe that little orphan is mute—wordless
as she is soulless, lifeless, even bloodless
because she is deathless.
They believe she can never die because she cut out
her death when her parents died of a wildfire,
she hid it in a diamond hidden in a seed
hidden in a heart hidden in her huge
auburn hare she is always with.
Townspeople sprinkle salt around her hut
while her death hops in the yard, then stands
on its hind legs, pricks its ears up, and watches—
pink nostrils move like it curses all over their lies.
They believe her death must be killed before it kills,
yet how could they know that death is a loyal
lover, eternal, that death itself is immortal?
They learn after many hares pour out
of many holes—merciless.

THE DAY WHICH WE FEAR

GAIL SCHULTE

The day which we fear as our last is but the birthday of eternity. —*Seneca*

Everyone is so afraid of death, but the real Sufis just laugh: nothing tyrannizes their hearts.
What strikes the oyster shell does not damage the pearl. —*Rumi*

The voice on the answering machine was soft, stoic. Dictated on a fast-moving
train.
    It's AIDS, you said. As if introducing a mysterious new friend.

I spasmed as I had the second before your birth, ran from the unspooling
words, dissolved into rolling, cross-hatching waves of pain.

I watched as the rose petals on my teacup exploded in slow motion,
scarring wall tiles, lemon tea staining the sink below a sickening yellow brown.

You, who gifted me pearls snatched from the silt of the Bali Sea,
so steady in this tsunami you've triggered—calm as the stone-hearted Buddha
you follow, levitating on the soft seats of a commuter train going... where?

You, who I expected would be the second coming of your father, only more
fresh
and comely, will widow me by proxy a second time, I fear.

. . . .

You would make me—who shined your shoes and parted your hair
with my own spittle—dress you in death.

Son, HIV, this selfish day, you would un-mother me.

    You would make me close your casket, like the door of an empty vault.

ALL HANDS

GAIL SCHULTE

Last night on the couch, I folded myself up, all angles, a stiff origami crane, and waited for the EMTs.

The clock leaked numbers in bright blocks. No weighty pinecones on chains, scavenged from the Black Forest floor, as I once imagined. No cuckoo playing hide and seek with time.

Crickets.

I sensed my bowels beginning to give way, relieved—this is the true word—for the plastic beneath my behind. Mom, harried, never hovered over her children. Ever. But her voice calms me now: *We may be poor. But we will be clean.*

At 12:15, I recalled finding Muriel Rukeyser's note, penciled in that strong hand, tucked among her thinning papers at the Library of Congress:

> *The thing is, I was born.*

The Sirens drew close at 12:32. No need to stir and rouse the cat, sleeping under the bed.

The thing is, when they lifted me from the couch, everything fell away, time dangling, weightless.

LEAVE ME THE LIGHT

JENNIFER WEIGAND

My back bakes,
cooked by the swath of sunlight
streaming in from the window.

I could stretch,
but then I'd disturb you.

Clear, hollow lines
attach to
your leaden limbs.

You're sandwiched
between a cumulous cloud
of scratchy blankets
and the hospital mattress.

I should have hung
that crystal.

Your breathing falters,
ceases.

My core dims,
shreds.
The room blurs.

No.

I could have gathered the shards
of your soul
as it fractured
into rainbow pigments.

If only
I could imprison them in my heart,
forever holding
the prismatic sunlight
that was you, my love.

MAPLE LEAVES

DANUTA K. KOSK-KOSICKA

On a wind-singing day
I wade in the red-leaf drift.

Sunny yellow, knee-deep, they dance
when I walk with you at seventeen.

In a story book the last leaf
hung on a maple tree
by her father
keeps a sick girl
from going away with the leaves.

With a hand-written quote
from your favorite poem
praising the art of living
you chose to go away
when flocks of leaves still hang on.

Fall after fall.

VACUUM

DANA GILLAN

I go to your room
even though you're not there…
I just want to hold the doorknob—
remember the feeling of you behind it.

WITNESS

ELLI SAMUELS

So much time has passed. Unplanned,
I go there again, dreaming backwards.

Wondering about mother love
—the fissures, missed kisses.

Years of tears glazed on her cheeks,
me arched in tight space.

What is there to say to a mother
betrayed, knotted as lichen?

Pups crying for suck had me thinking
—about bruised earth, erosion, the motion of hope.

That fog has its reckoning, how you must
hunt down the source. Eat wisely.

This thing that I learned about telling,
is truth can be taken down

from a vine-covered fence and re-trained to speak fully.
A time frame can be cushioned with blur.

Somehow—someone can die in the middle.
Still—make milk.

VERISIMILITUDE

TERRI WATROUS BERRY

The early sun comes callously across the pane,
laying on hands, one that holds this pointed pen
transfusing words into a page.

I've not yet begun to write, the hand exposed
exclaims *No!* The skin cannot already be
this slack, these blue and swollen riverveins

surely will recede—perhaps in spring?—
bring alabaster answers back to
the quivering question of my tenuous time.

But the light stares down denial, quickening this
stranger's hand, this hand that's held the pages of
my plot, already foreshadowing the denouement.

MORE QUESTIONS THAN GALAXIES

MOUDI SBEITY

I bet there are more questions than galaxies in the universe
said the nine year old sifting orbs of sand through his fingers.
Yes, I repeated, slowly savoring his declaration on my tongue,
I bet there are more questions than galaxies in the universe.
Just what draws a child to ponder their imagination beyond
the ridiculous and into the poetic. Beyond the fantastical and
towards the poignant and real. Like a little Rilke, this one,
living the question. So we are made by the possible. And in
order to continue being, in order to continue our breath as felt, there
must be a large region of unanswered fertility that makes up the
universe, that holds all of the galaxies in it. More space than matter.
More darkness than objects for light to bounce off.
So there is more potential than we have so far realized. More
undiscovered than discovered. More soil than trees.
There is more curiosity than certainty, he is saying.
More mystery than known.

"MY MEMORIES—THEY WERE LIKE STARS"

JOANNE HARRIS ALLRED

—after Louise Glück, "Midnight"

If I could pick one memory to relive,
I might choose the afternoon
driving beside scorched rice fields, Julie
riding shotgun and her partner, A. M.,
leaning in from the back seat. It's after Thanksgiving
that year of the fire, and the ashes—tiny particles
of trees, houses, and burned up animals—have diffused
into a sapphire sky. What leads to A. M. telling
the dream of her father dying?
She watched him detach from his body
and lift toward limitless sky
as shimmering images sifted off
his dissolving form,
each a glinting mirror
of a moment, a memory, like diamonds
dazzling a lake before sundown.

Were those images a stripping
or an offering? Only beautiful ones?—
like that morning snow-shoeing
in the silent Wisconsin woods
when he spotted a scarlet cardinal on a white
branch, and elk moving behind bare trees.

This time I'd pull over, shut off
the engine, turn to listen more deeply.
Were the fragments holograms
of what he had loved, his daughter's
young face among them? Still so many
questions. I'd like to know if her dream
came true when, a few years later, she faded out
in a patch of tall grass leaving
the night sky sparked with memories.

A MATTER OF TIME

KELLY MILLER

The cabin was alight with the glow from the fireplace. Martin sipped from his mug, the steaming herbal tea warming him from the inside out. Since Patty died, he spent nights like this—watching the flames dance on the logs, tending the coals until his old knees couldn't sit anymore, losing himself in the past.

He stirred, and Georgia lifted her head from the fraying rug to look outside. Her floppy ears dusted the floorboards, black muzzle sniffing the air.

"Go back to sleep, ol' girl." He rubbed at the greying stubble on his chin that matched hers. "It's just the storm."

Georgia whined, looking out the window before reluctantly lowering her head.

Martin stood, his joints giving way to multiple cracks and pops. He placed a hand on his lower back and groaned. "Ugh. I'm gettin' old, Pat," he said to the pink urn on the mantle.

He knew what she would say. She'd tell him to quit whining, quit drinking, and to exercise more.

Hell, she was right. "You were always right."

Wind pelted snow against the cabin's walls, piled it high up on the windowsills. Winters here weren't for the weak; theirs was the only house for nearly fifty miles. Just wilderness, far as the eye could see. A great place to live out the rest of your life.

He never expected to do it alone.

The front door blew open with a loud bang, startling him enough to drop his mug. It shattered, sending shards of glass flying across the room. Georgia jumped up and started barking at the wind.

"All right, all right. Enough." He walked to the door, bracing himself against the harsh, whistling gusts biting at his cheek.

Georgia barked endlessly, nearly drowned out by the roaring winds. Martin pressed against the door with his whole body, with all his might, but it wouldn't shut. When he stepped back, the door flew open, knocking him in the head.

"Shit," he said, rubbing his temple. "Damn it, Georgia. Stop bar—"

Movement at the tree line caught his eye. Georgia bared her teeth, growling low and primal.

Martin shushed her. "Easy, girl."

With the curtain of snow falling, it was hard to see what, or who, it was. From where he stood in his doorway, it was a few hundred yards away.

But getting closer, he realized.

Georgia took a step forward.

"No," he commanded. "Stay, Georgia."

She looked as if she may listen. Considering it, she lowered herself halfway into a sitting position, before leaping off the porch in a single bound and running off.

Because whatever it was, it ran right toward them. And Georgia ran to meet it, sprinting and snarling.

"Damn," Martin hissed under his breath. He looked at Patty's photo, at her warm smile, and thought about what she would do.

With a sigh, he grabbed his coat off the hook, threw his rifle over his back, and stepped into his boots as quick as he could, his muscles stiff and weak. After a lull in the breeze, he managed to pull the door closed, donning his gloves as he ran.

She was just up ahead, running straight for the shadowed figure emerging from the forest. The size of it started to become clear—huge, with loads of fur.

His knees protested as he tried to run faster. "Georgia!"

The hound kept barking, sights set on her target and gaining speed quickly. That's when Martin saw it—a giant grizzly sprinting on all fours.

He froze. Shit. I can't fight a damn grizzly, he thought. "Georgia! Get your ass back here!"

If she knew it was a bear, she didn't show it.

Martin pulled out his gun and looked down the sight, but it was a whirlwind of claws and teeth. The two collided in a frenzy of brown and black fur, thudding to the ground and sending a plume of snow up into the air.

A small cry called out over the raging storm, so quiet he could barely hear it. He stilled and turned his eyes from the brawl, just for a second, and saw a bear cub looking right at him. *Her baby.*

Instantly, he crept toward it, and to his surprise, it crawled to him. He scooped it into his arms and did the one thing he could do. He prayed to God for courage, and to Patty for forgiveness, then raised it up high by the back of its neck until it yelped.

The mother dropped Georgia with a sickening blow, then, to his horror, thundered toward him.

But all he could see was Georgia laying too still behind the bear, a thick pool of blood staining the snow around his dog, his best friend.

Tears welled in his eyes as the grizzly closed in, the baby's cries echoing in the night. Its mother let out a menacing roar, and once she was close, Martin tossed the cub to his right, safely onto a pile of snow far away from him.

He took off after Georgia, limping the whole way and not looking back.

"Georgia!" he called out. But she didn't move.

When he finally got to her, her breaths were shallow and too far apart. She tried to stand, but immediately fell back down, blood gushing from a wound in her leg.

"Georgia, what the hell? Why'd you have to go and do that?" He sniffled, a few of his tears falling on her soft fur.

Despite the cold, he shrugged off his jacket and wrapped her in it, prepared himself to run for the cabin. But as he did, her body went sickeningly limp, and Martin's heart dropped.

"No," he said, shaking her. "Come on, now. Don't leave me, Georgia."

But Martin knew in his heart that he was too late. His body had failed him. Had he gotten to her sooner, maybe he could've sa—

The unmistakable roar of a grizzly boomed behind him, so close her breath was warm against his back. He grabbed his gun and whipped around, pointing a trembling barrel right at her.

She snarled, seething and drooling, ready to shred him to pieces for touching her cub.

Martin cocked his gun and kept it raised at her. And they stood, man and mother, staring into one another's souls.

He counted to ten. Then twenty. Still, the bear waited, as if waiting for him to decide. Until, after what seemed like an eternity, she averted her gaze to the dog on the ground behind him.

Quickly, he moved to protect Georgia's body, trying to make himself seem bigger than he was.

It was a feeble attempt, but the bear's attention faltered when her cub ran up to him and sat, sniffing his pants.

With tears streaming down his face, Martin lowered his gun.

His wife was dead. His dog was dead. He might as well be dead too.

He dropped to his old knees, right beside Georgia, and wept. All the tears he'd held in for a decade, he let them all come, here, right before the end. He cried so hard, he barely heard the soft footsteps of a mother and her cub walking back into the forest.

He buried Georgia behind the cabin, beside Patty's favorite tree.

That night, he sat by the fire and sipped on whiskey. His hands were bloody and calloused from hours of digging into frozen ground.

Flames licked up from the hearth, reflecting flickering golden light off the buckle of a pink collar hanging off the mantle.

"So," he said to a room full of ghosts. "It's only a matter of time."

GROOM

MARY M. BROWN

Harold would rather be
        in heaven, among the angels,
his much-missed Ruby one

of them, he knows. He knows
        he shouldn't long for death,
such longing in conflict with

his long-held strict theology:
        this life on earth God's gift
to us and not to be eschewed.

A godly eschatology cannot
        be challenged or denied, but
still, still as he shaves, looks

in the mirror, parts his thin
        hair, he longs for her, his angel
Ruby, bride of sixty-five years,

not counting those after death
        that parted them like a comb.

IN THE MORNING, BEFORE I DIE

HALEY EDWARDS

My pasture goes to seed,
chickweed balm, buttercup jewels,
one stalk at a time,
summer's lacy last carrots.
Wisdom shocks me hair by hair.
Take me to my God,
lay me in the ragwort field.
Some of His best work:
pink of my skin in sunlight,
baldness of the black buzzard.

FALLEN LEAF

STACEY FOILES

The winding arroyos here
do not compete with the trails
we raced—so surefooted.
Valiantly leaping from
toppled pine
to jagged granite
Weaving our path beneath
flickering aspens to reach
our own Fallen Leaf
where the water is crater deep.
We take turns rowing
splashing that black water
against our silver boat.
It was all Saturdays for us
back then.
A mile of running and two of rowing
for a bag of M&M's
swiftly swallowed
before we caught our breath.
I scattered your burnt body
from there to here
50 years ago.
Now, I imagine
you looking
with your crooked eye,
Accusing me of taking
more than my share.

DRINK THE OCEAN

ANNE RAMALLO

Life can be broken
fast as porcelain.
Nothing to do but live—
eat, kiss, make poetry.
I embrace the dirt and bugs
and one day I'll give my soft self to them
with an ocean in my belly.

OF DEATH & DAISIES

SIERRA TAYLOR

Nothing will delight me more,
when I am laid to rest deep within the earth,
than the thought of little old me,
pushing up daisies.

Of wildflowers, violets, bits of clover,
sprouting from where my body lies,
my body blooming, what a marvel, what a joy,
for I have always loved all things that grow.

If from me springs a garden,
something green, something ripening,
if I were to become daisies,
to think of death as a sweet leafy sleep,
on a literal bed of roses, well—
I'm looking out the window,
at the flower patch planted by my husband.
I am not afraid.

MADE FROM MIDNIGHT

KELLY MILLER

Death is the song that sings at twilight,
when dreams start to fade with the waning sun,
when beating hearts slow and threaten
to break, to burn, to halt;
where once beautiful things dance
underneath pale shrouds and shriveled hands.
The graveyard comes alive with it,
that music that reminds,
while the conductor of eternity
dons a gown made from midnight
and twirls their fingers in a chalice full of fate.
There is nothing left to do but wait.

REMEMBER MY MELODY

TINAMARIE COX

Life withers away so beautifully
and slowly.
Garden verses play
with the sweet fullness of a symphony,
and then, all of a sudden,
we are found at the end.
Full stop.

We collaborated on an adagio tune
winding through the numbers
as we waited to dry out,
to lose color,
to wrinkle, and then yield.
Our music finally dissipates.
Caesura. We part. Your solo.

Tell me you'll remember this flower's song
long after the bloom is shriveled and gone,
and the rich shade of green, that
mark of vibrancy in life,
has faded quietly.
Full stop.

INSTRUCTIONS TO THE STUDENT UPON RECEIVING MY BODY FOR DISSECTION

E. LAURA GOLBERG

Here's this lived-in shell of nerves and organs,
empty of soul, just sinews of life remaining.

Mark muscles succumbed to rigor mortis,
then forever relaxed, hands I wrote with,
stilled, breasts drooping, silent as to their fondling.
Label each bone: *tarsal, metatarsal, fibula.*

See my feet, reliable in their plodding action,
thousands of miles walked in their time,
telltale scars from bunionectomy.

Find the line on my left inner thigh with dots around it,
formed when my sister, five years' old, sprang
on the headless rocking horse, pushing me forward
so the sharp broken hinge sliced deeply—white drops
of fat showing in my blood. She thought she'd killed me.

Then cut, expose those, oh so reliable, heart and lungs
that pumped and breathed, enriched blood cells,
stomach, that engine of digestion, worked on so many meals
to fuel the whole enterprise.

Can you spot the white band on my left ring finger,
exposed to the sun after 40 years of married life?

Find the tongue that curled round words,
the brain firing as eyes spotted *lugubrious, syntactical.*

Take what you've learned from me, apply it to others.
That will be my immortality.

CLINIC DAY

KATHY PAUL

Mom carries a folder, trails paper
in her wake. The bones of her hands
flutter from clipboard to wig—the bones
of her face are ghastly, like knives.

She muddles and slurs, pours
a clatter of cards from her wallet:
You please find it,
you know the right one.

Once again, we confer over questions,
dates she doesn't remember, lists of symptoms
and signs, bodily functions she addresses
with little girl words:
Tummy trouble. Tinkle.
Number two.

We are here to discuss the options for another
round of chemo. *I have cancer?* she
says in disbelief. She bats her eyelids
at the doctor: *I can't button my britches,* she says.
I think I ate too many Snickers Bars.

SHELTERING

STELLA STOCKER

In this sunken place there is no ticking clock.
Time paces back and forth, amber colored
and winged, cradling larva between
their mandibles. In all this fear, only the past
stands still.

My mother clears cobwebs from the wooden shelves,
stacked with seeds and dust jackets.

Light tumbles down the stairs, just enough
to pretend that day is breaking, that the sun is rapping
politely. Now I am cutting my hair—just like my mother's—
a confusion of curls giving way to shaved fields.

This moment has left and I am descending
into childhood's dim slips of memory.

I am picturing all of the worst and best things up there: that cities
have crumbled to ash and sextons are stooping to dig,
that cities are cosseted by ivy and morning glories.

Sparrows proselytize outside, singing a hymn
older than themselves.

Here the underground people are quiet.
Here I am kissing the corners of this silence hoping
it opens into sound.

I wish I could find my mother's hand to hold but
she is fluttering away somewhere in the corners.
I splay my fingers on the packed dirt and wait
for vibrations like a spider tweaking a silk line.

An end is coming soon, I can feel it.

THEY DIED DOING WHAT THEY LOVED

CAROL DAVIS

their friends said.

Isn't freefall a kind of death to begin with?
Dressed in squirrel suits; arms stretched into wings,
their faith, the certainty of wind that sweeps Yosemite.

We have all wanted to fly, but in dreams I never
maintain height, dip dangerously low over choppy waters.

If selection favors genes with an aversion
to danger, how did Dean Potter and Graham Hunt
ignore the natural reaction to fear?
Is it the same hunger to gape at car accidents?

What of Lot's wife (the humiliation of never being named)?
Was it Sodom she longed for, a life of guarantees?
Punishment for barring the angels from her house
or the two daughters in the doomed city.
Still, how can a mother abandon her children?
One last look.
A decision.
An impulse.
The neck turning slightly, only one eye to see
what she left behind.

A DEATH KINDER THAN LIFE

WENDY CHAPPELL

on the 7th day of her dying
i long-walk the beach in the late morning,
early april sunshine brilliant and blinding.
the restless north atlantic
worries the shoreline, etching ECG tracings
in the fresh, smooth stretch of sand,
freckled with kelp mounds and bits of lobster traps.

i collect seashells.
fingers trace gratitudes in the wet sands
as i harvest.
my hands redden, exposed
by my drawing in prayers.
what i begin without plan or intention
moves me, guides me,
shakes and spins me, dances me,
into a howling-loud, messy scene.
there is no one to see me, as usual,
but these moments neither need
nor want witness.

on the 2nd day of her dying,
Every Single Emotion
had gloved up and entered the ring.
here in this clarifying air, i unglove.
in the lick of ocean's salty spray
i welcome every sensation, embrace their pulse and crash,
feel them rise up, take form as whitecaps
and throw themselves upon me.
surely, there must be peace
amidst this slug and tangle
where no ropes catch my flung body.

a stone the color of sun-bleached seaweed
shot through with veins in shades of shame and sorrow
glistens on the sand,
glossy and smooth like raw cardiac tissue,
hard and unyielding like her heart.

the stone in my palm offers itself.
is it the hand of a dying mother?
i clasp it to my heart and step into the ocean,
the tug of sand under my feet as the waves recede—
the earth pulled out from under me.
i am the ocean,
fluid and shifting—
shifting and shifting.

all that has come to her, through her,
generations of festering wounds
in iterations of maimed childhoods,
lacerations that were never licked,
coping skills that hardened into
the fortress she became,
seasoned her armor as one would
season a cast iron
forged so hot and furious
no crack would ever allow
light to shine through.

all of it here now,
has arrived in me
on this april morning,
the 7th day of her dying.

the stone, now a poultice on my heart,
absorbs it. all of it. welcomes my burdens.
i hurl the stone, heavy with ancestral poisons.
it carves a high arc into the sunlight, over the waves,
and settles with a soft plunk.
barely a splash, it cut the devil's throat.

at home again, lighter
i sidle up to her bed and find her
animated for the first time in many days,
eyes bright and speech clear,
her color a glowy golden.
she is, surprisingly, sweet. sweet!
a word i would never have used to describe her
before today.
perhaps this is our parting gift to each other.

DEATHWATCH

KATHY PAUL

When I knew I should be
asleep, even when I knew the
overnight aide's knock was
inevitable, I binged on small-screen
violence: a handsome and incongruous U.S. Marshal
doing incongruous things handsomely.

Vaguely aware of the inappropriate
level of bloodshed tonight of all nights,
I devoured until my eyes burned: his sweet caramel
drawl, the seductive glitter
of his badge, his eyes.
I gorged on relentless gunfire.

The certainty of fictional death
blunted my fear of its all too real
visitation across the hall.

With one finger I traced
the contours of the Marshal's lips,
the outline of my hips,
even as I waited for the knock
I dreaded, the knock I wished would come.

Exhausted, I sank into the screen,
escaped by narrating
myself in the third person:

> *<<She left one earbud dangling, in*
> *order to hear the inevitable knock*
> *when it came.>>*

Even now, I am allowed
only flashes of remembering—
I catch no glimpse of myself
bending to kiss
my mother's skeletal cheek.

CAMELLIA

LAUREL BENJAMIN

—after Georg Trakl's "Song of the Departed"

The light in the room leans to one side
and camellias out the window, their faces
wonder. The bush my mother stared through
these months as if trying to find the sky.
Sometimes when I visited she could still petrify
rocks with her glare until she laughed open-
mouthed, but mostly I waited for her to use
her right hand to hold a cup, anything.
When they gave up on her I fought.
Now, the chamber music I'd put on her disc player,
silent. Now, her forehead cool as a camellia
cascading, cantata with harpsichord and loosely,
the strings, what's meant as accompaniment
for voice joined with pinkness, a color my mother
never wore, instead the melting crimson fire
soloist, how she swept into a room and brought
the sky. Holding her hand I remember how she loved
the camellia bushes in our yard, said they competed
with the petunias for attention, how she loved the wide-
open spaces of canyons and soft bushes in spring.
The harmonics of birds. Now, death delayed
because no one wilts in an instant, one by one organs
once tender, rotting then shut. A ruby-crowned
kinglet alights on a branch, then before
the chorus it roams with joins, it flits off.
My mother will not wake again, forehead
cold, yet cheeks pink somehow as if
the camellias have slipped through the window,
possessed her, the room inflorescent.

SHE WHO CARRIED

KIERSTEN ANDERSON

A bed from 1989 with a broken leg
Musty sweaters in the back of the closet
Completed Sudoku puzzles from the paper
Pristine couches feigning the use of comfort
Chitlins unthawing in the sink
A for-sale sign plunged into wheat grass
Your walker in the trunk of my Toyota
Unworn heels kept in their boxes
Dried-out teeth on an ashtray
The croaks of water-damaged floors
Tattered pages of your Bible litter the halls
6-inch stilettos tiptoe to the altar
Mistful eyes admire your burial gown
Sons chain themselves to the headstone
A matriarch has fallen
Her people burn.

FOR MARILYN

MILLIE PERCIVAL

Shall we stay here forever?
To watch the waves rock back and forth,

> memories slowly being eroded by time
> washed away while cracks form

without anything but water to fill them.
Horizons empty without sunlit glow as

> when you were here, how was I to know
> about rose-tinted glasses and radiotherapy?

We sat cold beside coastal defenses after chemotherapy,
and now, I'm sat here alone by the same sea

> with a hollow tumor left in me.
> you've become my misplaced cell

phone, I'm waiting for contact.
I'll call by soon.

> For now, I'll rest on earthen ground
> in a world where you're not around.

Corrosive brine slips down from my eyes
and I do not understand death.

THE FUNERAL

MILLIE PERCIVAL

It was early morning
and we moved like an insect.
Black shells, twitching limbs,
huddled together shuffling onward.
We move in sync with each other,
clinging onto arms and hands
so that another can't slip away
and be carried along before us.
We must carry ourselves along.
The sky's somber hues of gray
spilled through the slices of trees
as we marched through the mud
that gasped for air beneath our boots.
It was still early mourning that day.
Our watery eyes and aching souls
held onto the last vision of you
until finally it was time to leave
and for you to rest.

MOURNING

TINA PARKER

Wearing mourning dress
SEE SACKCLOTH
cutting or plucking off the hair and beard
SEE BALDNESS
covering the head and face
Laying aside ornaments
Walking barefoot
Laying the hand on the head
Ashes put on the head
Dust on the head
Dressing in black
Sitting on the ground
SEE MOUNTAIN

PART THREE

Dirty Feet

LOST

RENEE FEGAN

Drinking down
death. Falling
into dreamless sleep
Moments lost,
hours lost, days
lost, time
slipping
away into incoherent
darkness. Enveloped
by nothingness,
a void of ceasing
to be.
The world and
I no longer
tangible, no longer
corporeal.
Pinned down by
the weight
of everything
and
nothing.

ON WEDNESDAY

J.N.V

I cooked one egg
and I listened to birds
recite the morning chaos.
I didn't sleep.
Even though I tried.
I just kept
wishing
for something other
than this
something other than
the light fading from your eyes
and the dust settling on all of my favorite things.

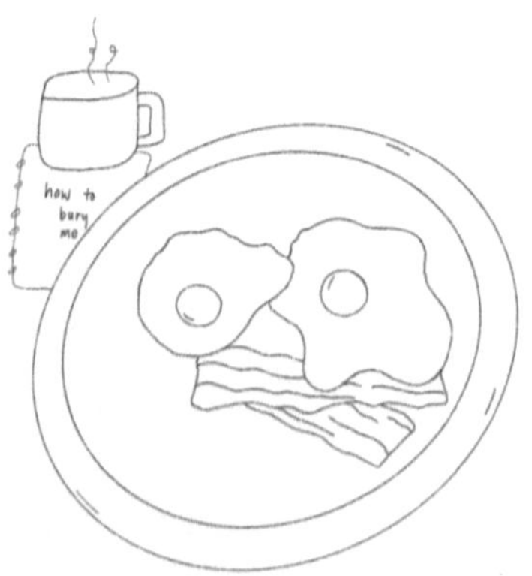

IN MY MOTHER'S HOUSE

KATHY PAUL

I would have killed for sleep
if so much death had not already
seeped under closed doors, drifted
even through keyholes.

Suffocated, I keep the night
watch, waiting with unfamiliar
shadows. I become another ghost now

accustomed to drift on noiseless
feet across the cold tile, staring
through the dark to the place
fifteen steps from the door

where her bird feeder holds
vigil, waiting for hands
that will not bring the seed.

STRANGE ARCHITECTURE

STELLA STOCKER

My ears are weakened teacup curves,
stained by the life that filled
this house for years.

My father's voice had arched around corners and
when he sang, the house vibrated like a bee
humming in a flower's throat.

Sun didn't enter the room, it was the room.

Now an echoing ache shakes
rafters to foundation. The air is stale and sweet,
like fruit turning.

Spider plants watch from their webs.
My sneaker lays on its side, its tongue lifting
words that fall flat on the floor.

His pile of journals and Vonnegut paperbacks
are loved even in forgetting.

Pages have loosened from their spines,
same as a body becoming undone in a casket,
starved for touch and movement.

JUGLONE

KATIE BYRUM

With you in a box, when I finally came back to box up
the life you left in our childhood home,
across the street was Maud on her porch
in her Keds, her roller-set curls (now gray) tight as ever.
Maud, one of those sturdy holler women
who outlived her husband,
who mowed the lawn til she was eighty-seven,
and whose children had to hide her car keys because By god,
there were cans of peaches and washing soda that needed bought.

I toddled into her driveway, the same path
I'd laid at eight years old with messy hair and muddy sneakers
offering to help gather up walnuts or hang the laundry
(to be kind to my elders, of course, and definitely not
hoping there might be an ice cream sandwich in the freezer).

When she saw me, she called me by your name.
I, looking as nothing like you as I've ever looked,
let the sting sit for a second, welling my eyes.

When I corrected her, her face changed:
awakened by surprise, then, warm as cobbler
she exclaimed my name back to me
and suddenly, I was eight years old again, with tooth-fairy holes in my grin.

I had her for twenty more seconds: Where were my folks living now?
The sting again as I said "well, you remember—"
and I realized, when she frowned, that she didn't, and couldn't.
A few more words and the light dimmed out,
put her eyes far away, and she was back to a loop
restarted each time she forgot her words.

I told her goodbye on the third But still I'm thankful to the lord,
and by August she was gone, too.
But I bet there's at least one bobby pin
somewhere in that soil
black as the walnuts that stained our hands.

ABOUT A MOTHER//PULL OF LANDSCAPE

CAROL DORF

we forgot to ask

remaining rooted

marked endpoints

while the winds swirled

tried as we could

to shield our eyes

recorded questions

fragments of earth

to remember her

at the gravesite

answers and hesitations

one bent tree

at the event horizon

we held distance

until night broke

until the storm faded

as if we stayed

as if we blew off

in multiple times

like seeds in the wind

WYOMING

TINA BARRY

I don't think much about ghosts,
except the one in that old hotel in Wyoming,

where my husband snored off our dining room dinner,
steak a la bland, no salt. *You poor sufferer*,
I told myself. Ordered a cocktail at the bar,

swirl of pearly green, pooling,
a spirit, frothy in a glass.

Mahogany counter long as a ship, phony
lanterns, and a mixologist twirling his moustache,

who spoke of spooky sounds only he could hear.
I don't think much about ghosts. But today,

when light poured a swirl of pearly green,
a pool on the wood floor I'll never dive into,
I recalled Wyoming and moustaches,

bad hotel dinners. My mother dead six months,
and why she never visits.

THE CROW WHO MOANS EACH MORNING

LAUREL BENJAMIN

keyhole shape high among the neighbor's
pines, a mother's feathers downcast, voice

unbound, like the first vowel of my name
elongated, a *Caaaaaw* my mother prolonged

to defeat my cause. Was I born a crow
to injure her? This afternoon the garden

is awry with cries—jukebox mix
of country western seagull and an operatic

bass crow—when the needle
falls suddenly on this scene to silence.

I don't breathe.

My story layers over this mama of shine and wisdom,
mama of spirituals, teeth clenched in rhythm

to a warning against intruders. I'm no mother,
but rise my *Caaw* to feathers plucked. It's already

April when chicks hidden *Peep* in the jasmine.
We are all bound up with impending

change, the crow's story a heartbreak ballad,
message redux inside her forehead or maybe

she's overthinking the steps and stages
for becoming a mother. Afternoons, she weeps

to the magnolia tree, talons gripping knobby
branches, flapping in the small space between

brown blossoms, displacing sparrows and towhees
who must land in low bushes or perch

on woven chairs. Is it the curse of absence,
how loss incurs loss, or absence measured

by wingspan, plumage, iridescence.

DRAW NEAR

KIERSTEN ANDERSON

One year ago, they buried her. Locked the casket and walked away.
It was impassive, ritualistic:

"May God keep them in the hollow of his hand"

Sleeping has become bittersweet—tortured by her phantom caress
I dream desperate for expired warmth.

Trapped in a state of numbness, I let the sorrow feed.
Let it devour the burnt edges of joy.

Oh, how loud is the weeping of the forsaken rings.

Grief keeps me on my knees, and your Lord bows my head.
Brokenness is the backbone of faith.

Cauterize my heart with a match. No one moves on free of hurt.
Regret is a filth that stains.

Daily, I shed this love like skin.

WALKING OVER THE 10th STREET BRIDGE

KAYLA SARGESON

—for FUMO

It's the first of September and my grandmother calls
to tell me her cousin's husband died.
They were married 72 years.
I've spent the past two thinking about moving to Savannah,
but there's something about the brown water of the Monongahela
that keeps me here, something grounding in the dirt, the smoke blowing
from whatever factory is still operating across the river.
I look for the graffiti tags like old friends: AWAKE, KURU,
FTC, RIP DOK, SKITZO (who I think is in jail
in New York).
In Savannah, there's nothing to hold onto.
I float on dry land, cling to men who are just as slippery,
say I love you in the clichéd, moonlight way.
I don't know how people stay married for 72 years—
or why.
Last night I looked up "how to forgive" on the internet—
nothing new there—
so I move through the Armstrong tunnel like I'm undercover,
cross the bridge with dirty feet, dirtier heart.

MAYBE A BONE

KAYLA SARGESON

You call me at work to tell me how
on Saturday, you saw Cage The Elephant
at the social club on Tybee
and they weren't very good.
Outside the window where I take your call
a gray bird lies on a small roof patch,
its body concave where it shouldn't be.
That sucks, I say, *oh my god.*
The bird must have flown into the window.

You sold weed to the lead singer of the band,
suppose you could have upcharged him.
Uh-huh, I say.
My heart beats with the bird's quick breaths.
I could tell you that I love you.

Oh shit, my sandwich is here. Gotta go, you say,
and that's that.
I walk back down the hall,
sit behind my desk.
What was that about? a coworker asks.
Nothing.

I don't hear from you again for a week.
This time there was a shooting in downtown Savannah.
The bird's body turned into a home for insects,
will be nothing but dirt in two weeks,
maybe a bone remaining.

FEATHERY WORDS

DANIEL EDWARD MOORE

In the dream the ground told the tree
          you can only have two branches,
               which left the ground covered in birds
                    from nowhere to build their nests.

I'm not afraid of nightmares,
          except those stuffed with feathery words
               like "'til death do us part."

But which is better is hard to decide,
          the ugliness of weeping or
               the tears themselves?

In the dream Kleenex was too soft
          to be redemptive, too worn thin by crippled vows
               pretending they could help the soul
                    soar where nothing flies.

LOVE LOST

RENEE FEGAN

You drown me
in wells of deep blue.
My heart wrapped
in mourning ribbons tight
like Death's corseted waist.
Waste
of breath, waste
of light that filters through
charred and ashen bones
of a forgotten love.
You drown me
in a sorrow that sinks me
into the billowing
smoke of despair,
gasping for air, clutching
at tattered hope,
clutching my chest, my waist.
Waste
of time, waste
of thoughts bogged
in the mud of loss.
You drown me
with the presence of
your absence.
You drown me.

ELEGY FOR WHAT NEVER WAS

KIERSTEN ANDERSON

I loved him alone. Decades of helpless desire.
When he appeared. Appeared in my dreams. In
a faded sweater with thick eyebrows. When he appeared
I waited for the angels (nothing) and smiled (nothing)
and pretended to be a woman with standards.
I burned the manufactured mistress and he walked toward me.
His heavy steps had me writhing against the pavement.
Touch me. Don't stop. Mine. Man of my prayers.
When the dream ends. When I get off the ground.
When I don't want to. When all I can talk about are the angels
that never came. That means I am alone. When I can't feel him.
At night. Under my soft thumb. His. Nothing.

BREAK UP

ALESA BERNAT

If I were to let go of you
like a tree in autumn shedding leaves
You could decompose, break up your bits
replenish soil—
consecrate the body as an insect habitat
lay your limbs a feast for arthropods
your mind, a meal for animals

FISH SWIM

KELLY MILLER

This is the way all things must end:
dirty nails ripped through soil and flesh
to get to the other side,
chased white lights through
tunnels and met headlights.
All confrontation must be this bloody
if done correctly. The filets of your body
will be enjoyed next to fresh salmon and lemon.
This journey is a delicacy often served in time machines.
What song will you sing at the turn of the last page?
What lies? What promises?
Are you begging for your life?
There is something I'm sure
I'm forgetting to tell you;
everything melts away now.

WHEN MORNING CAME

JOYCE HAYDEN

When morning came the news was still true. Dreams had taken
reality away. I woke up with the death certificate in my hands.
I hadn't felt this shocked learning from Google that you had died.
The certificate arrived so innocently in a white envelope the previous
day, and now I couldn't keep myself from flying to the ceiling. I couldn't
get out of bed. I had to get out of bed. My sister was visiting and I was
driving us to the Grand Canyon. I pulled myself from the blow up mattress,
looked out the window, saw my sister below me on the patio, drinking tea
as barn swallows flew back and forth above her head. I packed the car in a
daze, stopped for gas. Drove from Cochiti to Albuquerque to Gallup and
Winslow and into the eastern gates of the canyon. My hands white knuckled,
glued to the steering wheel, the only thing still holding me to this earth. We
pulled into our first overlook. We walked in silence to the rim. I left my
sister there with her camera and journal. I walked the path west through fog
until I found a flat spot where I could pound the orange rocks with my fists
and scream into the vast gap of the canyon. Hoarse from yelling, red from
roaring, I returned to my sister. We took a selfie, swallowed water from
metal containers and walked back to the car, back to the hum of its engine,
back to the real world.

DEATH JOINS ME FOR BREAKFAST

JOANNE HARRIS ALLRED

orders sausage with huevos rancheros,
a big appetite for one so wispy.
He could eat you out of house and home,
suck the foundation like a bone.
When he chews toast slathered with butter
his jaw clicks like a set of castanets
we're all compelled to dance to.
When breath slows and the heart stops
he'll go on doom scrolling
reading the post about a boy caged
in an unheated basement, starved
to thirty-nine pounds by god-fearing parents.
He keeps an eye on the kid.

Lately he visits too often,
leering at my sister. I don't like
the way she flirts back
saying over coffee she's written
directions for donating her body
and perhaps my friend whose Soleri bell
was stolen would like hers when she goes.
It knells from her patio.
I despise his intentions and sneaky ways,
the arrogant presumption.
Last night he shimmied into my bed
and lay stiff as starched sheets rasping
a lullaby about a girl he found lost
in the frozen woods and tenderly carried home.

CHERRY BLOSSOMS

JOYCE HAYDEN

My heartbeat was always the sound of your feet
walking away. Every Sunday night when dusk fell
when the curtains closed, when the weekend magic
came to an end, when I watched you pack your bag,
your fishing gear, the feathers and thread for tying flies,
when you turned the key in the ignition, your lights
snapping on, taillights disappearing up the driveway
and over the ridge. In the weeks after Stephen died
all I could feel was the cruelty of you leaving, of not
staying Sunday nights to hold me through the darkest
hours when grief grabbed by throat and twined its body
like a boa, around my bones, my chest, my heart. Is that
how you felt that night in late December when I told you
the chasm between us was no longer something I could
cross? I know it is how I felt again two years ago when
the death certificate came and the "cause of death" bolted
out of the small box: *gunshot wound to the head*. I felt that
cruelty again but this time it belonged to me. I saw a war
movie once where a single soldier was fleeing pursuit.
He jumped into a river and the river carried him like a
frantic mother far away until he floated on his back. When
he opened his eyes, pink and white cherry blossoms fell from
branches and covered his face. That's what I hope for you, not
that you burned with regret, not that you fought against your
decision, but that the calm of darkness flooded you and cherry
blossoms filtered through the air and from your kitchen ceiling
resting lightly on your chest, before your head, your
back slammed upon the worn yellow linoleum.

THE MOUNTAINS HOLD SO MANY

TINA PARKER

Stooped kneeling frog crawling
Burned crushed cut suffocated
Brought out dead
Never found

     Bodies

BEFORE RESURRECTION

ALISON STONE

Drunks drive down streets where kids play. Someone dies.
A white boy has a bad day. Someone dies.

Where race meets misogyny, a man walks
into a spa. Bullets spray. Someone dies.

It's not a hate crime if your victims turn
you on. Candles lit. Priests pray. Someone dies.

The farmhouse settles. Barn cats yowl and mate.
Hounds howl moonward. Mules bray. Someone dies.

Winter melts into spring. On Monday, no
gun laws are passed. On Tuesday, someone dies.

What is more tragic, never-uttered love
words stuck in throats, or the way someone dies?

Blue plus-sign on a stick. Cancer in blood.
A new baby's on the way. Someone dies.

Man down. The ambulance trapped. When traffic
or dumb drivers cause delay, someone dies.

Words are knives. "Grab her by the," "Kung Flu." On
our screens, in instant replay, someone dies.

You tell the oldest stories, Alison.
Someone's in charge. Someone's prey. Someone dies.

OUR GODS

BETH MIDDLETON

Slack-grinned kitty, asleep but for a dribble of blood. Did we lay you
on that wall? As a million buds lay buried beneath the black that we lay for the
car that broke your back? As we allow you to catch the rat, not the chick? As
we pluck your claws, obscure your instinct, adorn the neck we snapped? We the
wheel, the car, the road, the black crack the buds, the rats, the necks the backs.
Yes, we lay you on that altar.   Our Gods demand we do.

EASTER EVENING

J.M. SUMMERS

The hillside burns, argued
out, as are we. It is the
fag end of the holiday.
There was a face in the wood,
but the wood has been turned to
ash, the fancy you made of the
hunched shoulders, flaming
hair, the smoldering eyes.
We are hollowed out, still
waiting on the question mark
that is the empty tomb.
Are we regretful? Of course
yes, always, but for all
the wrong things.

GHAZAL

MJ GOLIAS

Ask how one becomes unsuitable. Ask how one abides in the forgetting.
Ask how one becomes mosaic fragments that collide in the forgetting.

Empty the pockets of the culprits. Fill them with glass bits.
I'll throw my red wine at the guilty who hide in the forgetting.

My heart has turned to remains, but I still hold onto my knives.
How can one refuse those who neglected to lie in the forgetting?

Left-over apologies descend into floor cracks, seep into past
promises that acted as a guide in the forgetting.

I am versed in some languages. When you say, "Maria, I have loved,"
which Greek word for love would you use that hasn't died in the forgetting?

MIDNIGHT SOUND

GLEN MARCHAND

Soft shaman flutes, to conjure up spirit. Neat cultural wilderness, to soothe an inner thief. To marvel at caves, or mind petroglyphs those leaping into superstition. Architectural atmosphere, years at self-destruction; to become hopes, an anxious task, standing in silence. Ever and anon, compelling aesthetic art those gray moments those seizing seconds—such reach, an altered response, most anything becomes psychical. To shift perception, faced by rapture, measuring motion. Some elements are static—as it was a drumbeat, a trombone, to flicker gently. Across frequencies—amounting to a conundrum, if honest, a crisis—days in a trancelike estate, weeks rebuilding. A soul gravitates and sees pieces of reality, not quite believing his thoughts. Each premise was miscalculated; it neither would cease or deny certain currents—to weave a philosophic peg, to dance legato, moving with sound.

THE HOUSE THAT REGRET BUILT

ELIZABETH HOOVER

The welcome mat read "repentance welcome"
barely visible on the doormat
as if spoken in a whisper.
I stepped through doorways framed with disappointment
down a hallway famed for worries.
Aged floral wallpaper peeling on the edges
of low ceilings.
The scent of burnt toast lingered in the kitchen
where countertops were still wet
from splashes of spilt milk.
Unsent letters sob
in locked drawers upstairs.
The attic moans mournfully;
it echoes through the throat of the chimney,
into the living room where all the plants have withered.
Flower petals crisp as ash, sprinkled,
like macabre confetti on side tables.
There are no mirrors.
It is only ghosts that come to stay here.
If you visit,
whatever you do,
don't
go in
the basement.

PLANT PERCEPTION

LINDA FREUDENBERGER

My house plants let go.
The orchid slowly lost her purple blooms.
My pothos dropped her shiny green
upturned leaves to the floor,
along with meandering vines.

They let go.

My dragon plant released
her long spindly brown leaves
one by one
as they slid off the stalks where he
heaved his final gasp.

They let go.

I brought him to the vet that morning.
My beloved Clancy improved
but suddenly took a turn,
convulsed, drew his final breath,
and passed in the kitchen,
body wedged between orchid
and pothos, his green tennis ball
inches from tiny, white paws.

They let go.
Now withered leaves fill my home.

HERE BE DRAGONS

KELLY MILLER

deep in the garden
underneath the peonies and azaleas
a dragon sleeps atop piles of bleeding pages
a monster born from smoke and bone

there are places even
inside ourselves
we dare not go
caves and shallow pools
too murky to enter
too quiet to trust

the garden of my memory
is tended by a woman
with a red lipstick smile
and a spade sharp enough
to silence the skeletons
hidden in her bones

BONE CHINA

MILLIE PERCIVAL

Just where shall I put my bones?
I wonder as I open the cupboard
should I stack them up in a tower
slot them in, snuggled together
overhead on the highest shelf
which is only occupied by dust?
Do I place them down neatly
separating the plates and bowls
nestling themselves into spaces
between the mugs to grow old?
I stare deep into that hinged box,
before I picked up my waiting bones,
cradling them together in my arms
clinging to them, holding my breath
and walking to the silent blender.
I force them in with a rigid clunk
and let out a final breath,
as the machine whirs back to life.
Crushing up and then grinding down
into a fine powder so soft, so light
to be cast out the window, into the night.

A DRIVING MOMENT WITH DEATH

YVETTE SCHNOEKER-SHORB

Do you see those buzzards
hover over nearby dreary hill,

there near stagnant water,
murky green, where brush

reclaims its place between
shallow ditches, broken rows

of long-ago degraded fields
that now yield nothing more

than a misplaced carcass,
a deer whose diminished body

some sympathetic passing soul
must have cleared off the road?

But the vultures know; they
circle over forgotten earth

once customized for profit,
pastoral remnants to the side

of endless traffic and above
which glide wild passers-by.

SUICIDE ATTEMPT, STINSON BEACH

JEANNE WAGNER

Desperate, the way she threw open the car door
—bolted—left its weight hanging like the last word
in someone else's argument, left it heavy on its hinges
—agape—while she, middle-aged woman, wearing
not just the wrong shoes, hard-heeled, squished on
the inside of the foot but lavender sweats over her
broad-brimmed buttocks. Sometimes the body sobs,
it sobs, and we behold it, the ungainly bobble of loosely
wrapped flesh, the fraught, rubbed-together thighs,
rounded shoulders, rack and ruin of bones shaking
themselves into some long forgotten, misbegotten motion.
Such a far-flung run, a series of stumbles, an ungainly gallop.
Whatever it was that failed to pursue her became a phantom
at her heels, baying *Your fault*, shaming her, chasing
her down the asphalt drive of the parking lot, over the rocks
and whipcords of kelp, across the sand where she crawled,
cold sucking at her knees, her palms, while she offered
herself up to the sea. But there was no Hiroshige-like wave,
only the lacy sprawl of low tide. Maybe there was never
enough of anything for her. The water didn't want her.
It kept rolling her back on the shore. The park ranger
arrived out of nowhere, as if he were in some B- movie,
looking too laundered and fit, following each step
in the rescue manual, coaxing her back, while she lunged
away as if each wave could not only bury her but christen
her too. *Christ*, someone shouted—*Hold onto her,
talk to her. Ask her who she is*.

CORPSE

When they find my body
will they know that it was queer?
That it was touched with
pleasure and violence?
That it was touched
there and there and there?
Will the lines be a map of mystery?
They won't know how hard I tried
when they find my body.
I think I chose this body.
If anyone can choose a body
from where we were before
first breath, first dawn.
Our bodies will all return
to The Earth.
How do you want
Her to greet you?

DANCING IN THE RAIN

BETH MIDDLETON

And the fish will whisper
"Doesn't she move well?"
As my bloated corpse
Sways with the tide

A LITTLE ANCIENT PROMISE

ANDREW ECKAS

He's crouched near the tide, flipping over horseshoe crabs, gentle and caring, unaware I'm walking the same shore we both tried to forget. There he is—Jake's father. He doesn't notice me. He's focused. Working with the same deliberate care he'd given his son. I stand still in the sand, the waves biting my ankles. *Turn around. Pretend to disappear like I wanted to all those years ago.* But this is how guilt works. It clutches its claws around your neck, forcing you deeper into the cave you've carved for yourself. He stands and brushes the sand from his hands, orienting himself. His eyes flick from seaweed to the breaking waves, to me. I think his eyes must be the saltiest thing on the beach. The same eyes that bore into me at the funeral and asked me to leave.

I hate the sound of water, an intrusion that pretends to soothe. I remember climbing into the boat to the sound of water, a few rum and cokes deep, vision blurry. The syncopated slap of waves marks the moment I held his head in my arms, his face blue, lips purple, eyes wide open. There, under the stars, I dragged him ashore, onto the sand drained of heat, cold and empty like him. That happened two years ago, almost to the day, and I still hate the way I can only think of my best friend collapsed and blue.

It's almost the Fourth of July now, and it's been six days since I've had any food. Since anything. I open the fridge to see which will waste away first, the expired cold cuts or me. Sometimes, I stand outside restaurants and let the salted, deep-fried aroma venting into the street hit my nose. A jolt to the system that food exists, that other people still enjoy it. I loiter outside sniffing long enough to remind myself I don't deserve it, or until a hostess asks me if I need help. I'm halfway to scurvy because nothing tastes right when you know he'll never share a meal again.

My psychiatrist sent me on a wellness retreat. Told me I needed sun, not sedation. A vacation. Movement. A little hunger if I could find it. Get back out into the world and work up an appetite, because it's this or a feeding tube.

So, I chose the Cape. The beach where it happened. Call it immersion therapy, or a sick admission of guilt. I call it the only thing left I haven't tried. Confront the past, my therapist tells me. But what if the past is like me, avoidant and unsure? You don't walk back something like that. You don't explain it away. A best friend, gone because you were drunk, stupid, and selfish. If I'm not that person anymore, wouldn't I feel like someone else?

It doesn't matter that I held his hand. Tried mouth-to-mouth. Listened to the waves crashing against the stillness, one heartbeat hoping for another. One life ended while another began to rot. That's the whole story.

A wave crashes ashore, its remnants rinsing the sand. His eyes are ripping into me. He has Jake's eyes. I find it endearing when a son resembles a father, but not today. The sharp bay breeze flattens my clothing against my skin, showing me for what I am—the walking scaffolding of something more. Of something better. To him, I'm another kind of creature washed ashore. The last thing he expected to find. The emaciated ghost who killed his son.

"What are you doing here?" he says with a gnashing jaw and tightened fist. His back straight, shoulders taut. On guard as if I'd stumbled over his son's grave. In a way, I had. He takes a heavy step toward me and sinks into softened, wet sand. Between us, an upturned horseshoe crab writhes on its back, spinning in panicked circles, legs twitching into thin air. At the sight, he loosens, his body unspools. I expected a curled fist to collide across my gaunt cheek. To receive the physical punishment to match the pain swimming in my head. But that's the other thing about guilt. It masks your perception, like the world makes eye contact with you through sunglasses.

He kneels and flips over the begging crab. Diligent and automatic, as if saving those archaic crustaceans held him back from the liquor cabinet. I want to say something, anything, but my mouth runs dry, my body tenses. He cuts through the silence. "You know these things evolved before the dinosaurs," he says, "despite eons to figure this place out they still can't outsmart the tide. It washes them onshore, turning the unlucky ones over, and they lay on their backs, in the hot sun, waiting to die." I say nothing. "Of course, you already know all this," he says.

I step forward, leaving wet prints that the waves will soon erase. He leans down and flips over another patient crab. It moves in an immediate dash back to the ocean to where it belongs. It leaves a peculiar trail of tiny tracks, and a deep ridge carved into the sand from its hardened shell. He leans to flip another but stops and faces me. "There was a storm last night, so there's more than usual. Give me a hand?"

A motionless crab lies on its back, shell upturned like some cruel joke. More of a living primordial shield of crawling armor than what you'd expect a crab to look like. I flip it over, and instinct kicks in. Clawing clumps of earth, it drags its drained body back to the water. Dehydrated, hurt, starving, it uses everything it has left to find its way home again. It pays no attention to the evolved ape that gave it a second chance.

"I've been coming to the Cape since I was a kid," he says, flipping another one over. He tracks its haphazard scurry back into the foaming water. "Every summer. When they crawl up onto the beach to look for a mate and lay eggs. Back then we'd leave them on their backs, legs squirming. I never thought to flip them over. I took Jake here a lot too. He always flipped them over. That's when I learned you could save some of them."
 The rolling slap of waves spills before us, washing clean the prints behind me, as if to undo my presence. Despite the grime of the ocean on his fingers, he bites his nails. Jake had the same nervous tic.

I go to flip a crab myself, astonished at the weight of it. It careens down and smacks against the sand, dead, and I'm back to that night when I rolled Jake over and he hit the sand with the same lifeless thud. Unmoving, gone. A moment of disbelief when you remember that even the invincible die. Whether a hundred-million-year-old species or Jake.

It happened the night we graduated high school. Jake chewed halfway to his cuticles when I convinced him that I'd driven the boat tipsy a hundred times before. While the rest of our class dozed off drunk to Jimmy Buffett songs, it came down to one last trip out on the water. One last youthful moment of adventure before we pulled out loans and started our eventual climb on the first rung of the corporate ladder. Jake didn't say no; he wasn't the type of guy to let someone down. He raised his red Solo cup and nodded. Beyond inebriated, I disregarded that Jake usually sat at the edge of the pool, legs dangling, shirt still on. Forgot that he wasn't a strong swimmer. Hell, no one's a strong swimmer with a BAC of .17, but adolescent confidence mixed with cheap liquor and a dose of peer pressure, and Jake climbed on board. I revved the engine. Smooth, no resistance, the boat cut through dark, still water, and in that fleeting moment, for the last time, I knew freedom. Jake stumbled from bow to stern, heaving, sick. I revved the engine, fast, thoughtless. I kept slicing across the wine-dark abyss. Before I knew he'd gone overboard, his throat seized, lungs let go, and the ocean pulled him under. Did he slip? Was it the rev of the engine that sent him drifting beneath the waves? Did he call my name? Now I'm forever trying to catch his voice when I know I can't hear it.

"My wife thinks I'm crazy for coming here," Jake's father says. "For burning my PTO at a place that caused us so much pain. But I like the horseshoe crabs. There's a simple exchange between us. I give it a second chance at life, but it can't give me anything in return. It just crawls back to the ocean, almost as if I were a lucky gust of wind." He wipes away a fresh stream of tears. He takes careful steps at the edge of the beach and flips a crab. We watch it crawl back into the lapping waves. "To it, and its four little brain cells, I'm just another part of the beach. Another part of what's beyond the waves. I'm more than me. Feeling like that helps."

Stretched across the beach, infinite dots of little upturned crabs dominate the shoreline. I try to flip another one, but it doesn't crawl home. It's already gone. Another dead one. Another flash of Jake. Its shell cracked open, the soft interior exposed, brine and biological slime oozed out. Flies scatter.

"No such thing as a peaceful end out here," he says. "You can't get to all of them. Some are meant to dry up on the beach, or get picked at by birds, you know? Some are meant to meet their end." He bites his nails and blinks through red, teary eyes. Waves break, and the water reels back. "It's strange," he says, "I think I know him better now that he's gone. I save one, watch it crawl back to the water, and for a moment, he's back."

I close my eyes, and the crash of breaking waves grows louder. I hit the sand knees first. No longer able to support myself. I topple over, face pressed against sand. The swash rushes in, filling my mouth, flooding my empty stomach with salt. Sand hits my teeth. I choke. Spit. My breath shrinks, ready to stop. He lifts me and drags me up the beach like a loose piece of driftwood. My feet carve two deep ridges into the sand. He props me up against an embankment, the sound of the waves smaller, quieter.

"Promise me you'll come back here," he says.

"What?" I say, choking up wet clumps of sand.

"Promise me you'll come back here every summer and save as many as you can."

I don't know what to say back. I cough. The heat of the sun sears into my thin, starving skin. A white murmuration of birds flutters overhead. They glide onto the shore and peck at the scattered corpses of the crabs left on the beach. Hundreds of free meals.

"Promise me," he says. "Promise me."

"I promise." I nod a few times to reassure him. To reassure myself. He chomps into the nail of his ring finger, but something changes. His face, compressed into a mass of wrinkles, smooths out, relaxes.

"I don't blame you," he says, "not anymore. But I did. Oh God, did I wish it had been you and not him. I wished you'd rot in your own hell for being so dumb, so careless. But Jake made his own choices, lived his own life."

I look at the scattered tapestry of life. These ancient beings stare at the infinite turquoise above and wait for death or a savior. Saving one doesn't matter when the eternal churn of nature runs its course. But maybe it's not about saving them all, maybe it's about making right on a little ancient promise that if you can help, you should help. And that starts with yourself.

DESPITE UNIVERSALS

YVEETTE SCHNOEKER-SHORB

It's hard to believe the universe
is drifting out of existence,
that our ever-whirling world
would be fine without us,
that humans are just another form
of guts and blood and sinew and bone,
nothing special but the type of stuff
so easily turned to ashes and dust,
crudely unbound in random violence
or on purpose—neighborhoods,
military, medical, morgue—
as the entropic universe continues
to expand, to witness indifferently
from without and even so from cells
within our own diminutive domains—
our bodies; it offends the sense of self,
undermines our species, our perceived
significance excruciatingly small,
and yet, apart from the darkest soul,
there are those who act like angels.

THE ANATOMY OF A LIE

ELIZABETH HOOVER

I found it lying
curled beneath a lace doily
pretending to be innocent.
It reeked of lilies and rust.
Scalpel in hand
I unzipped the silent sternum.
The flesh gave way easily
soft on its superficial surface.
It sighed—like it missed the sound
of its own voice.
Its spine was a rosary
of half-truths,
each vertebra a haunted whisper
strung on prayer wire
pulled too tight.
The ribs were ornamental—
gilded with plausible deniability,
hinged with rusted apologies,
cracked from the strain
of holding back.
Its lungs held the fog of half-finished sentences.
Thick with names it had swallowed
and never dared to say,
echoes of what it begged others to see.
The heart—
a shriveled thing
wrapped in cling film,
beating… still,
but only out of habit.

And the tongue?
Filed to a perfect point,
polished with charm,
stored neatly in its cheek
next to a list of alibis
written in runes.
I didn't weep.
I labeled the pieces.
Wrapped them in silk.
Tucked them into a cold metal drawer.
There was no family to contact.
No one to mourn.
Cause of death: reclamation.
It choked on everything I finally said out loud.

RUACH

CATHERINE MCNIEL

If God's Spirit is Breath
and Wind
then she is the one I feel at my back
pushing
like a woman in the throes of labor
pushing
and pushing
us forward
when we are motionless in darkness

These dry bones are lifeless
But
She is giving birth
in the valley of death
pushing
and pushing
her children
to plant goodness
seek redemption,
cultivate justice on this wreckage,
this scorched earth

The birth cry comes
after despair claims victory
prematurely

Only a laboring woman,
could enter the room of death
panting with the breath of God
pushing
and pushing
until
redemption cries out,
tiny, vulnerable
only a flicker but
alive.

INTERLUDE

Breath and Wind

IN THE NAME OF THE MOTHER

MOUDI SBEITY

bismillah al rahman al rahim
 in the name of Allah, the most merciful,
                    the most compassionate

Mercy and compassion share the
common root word for womb in
                    Arabic—*rahm.*
This is to say;
what mothered us into existence is
an unconditional, indefinable, infinite
expression of love, so vast and selfless,
so raw and ever-giving, it created us
within the chambers of its own fleshy
desire. So that no matter how far away
I walk in my seeking, still I find myself
tethered by this perennial pulse born
from the body of my mother, and her
mother's mother, all the way through
to a lineage of water and dirt—
                    this precious earth—
one tilting heart forged by a dream of
inimitable mercy and endless compassion,
the place from which everything begins,
the ground to which we all return.

AFTER-AFTERMATH

HALEY EDWARDS

2 months after tornadoes, Bowling Green working to pick up, rebuild—WDRB

Now Spring: roof guns echo
through the lines of twisted oak,
where once the steady, timeless peck
of Northern Flickers tapped—

we find them battered dead
in flower beds and piles of wreck.
A thousand tiny burials.
A thousand more to come.

How long before the seeds
inside their broken bellies bloom?
How long before the bluegrass blinks
with buttercups as stars?

CONSIDER THE SPORES

MOUDI SBEITY

Here you are, by no conscious choice of your
own. What you know is little, and what you
know how to do even less. No one has yet
been able to say what comes next, except that
you've already inherited loss as a guarantee.
Someone you love will leave. Another will die.
Somewhere you call home will one day no
longer be.

All you can claim is this stretch between first
inhale and last release. You will arrive at your
concluding breath with this final realization;
there is nowhere to go, nowhere to get to.
Just the raw pulse of blood through vein. Just
the testimony of this brief life as one possible
blossom in time. Now you must do something
with this, your life I mean, become someone
through it.

Look, you can believe whatever it is you want
to believe in. I won't convince you otherwise.
But consider now how spores crawl through
the wet earth only to return to it.

Consider, now that you are wise, that perhaps
awakening is just another name for letting go.
Perhaps enlightenment is nothing more than
your own heart suckling at the dark.
Perhaps there is no purpose, only the way
cool water slips fresh between your fingers,
only the way your feet beg at the earth.

SELF-FLAGELLATION

TOMI OJO-FAKUADE

Lord, I am every transgression you are sworn against.
In a room, I am the absence of light.
In a garden, I am anything forbidden.
On a tree, I am the decaying branch spreading its rot.

Still,
As the Hart panteth after the water, here I am,
Seeking more than the breath in my lungs,
Another favor I do not deserve.

I have mastered the language of pain—Abba,
Sorrow is a dialect I am fluent in.
Like Bartimeus, I am blind to your light,
Unlike him, my eyes are wide open.

In church, the clergy calls for prayer,
Says closed eyes are a shortcut to your throne.
I close my eyes to see the light.

ELYSIUM

CHRISTIAN CHASE GARNER

I throw back
three Extra Strength Tylenol
on an empty stomach, feeling
the dark, sickly pang on the drive
through a barebones town
to renew my license. I pass
the graveyard and think of death
in a way that is less fear and more melting
its complexities for my poems—
a caustic echo; a deconstruction;
a soundless, benthic touch as
the soul is scalloped clean.
The gravestones are oddly bare,
most likely dead men who drank
tap water, a savior's name culled
from their open mouths before flatline—
the men who spent their youth
married to concertina wire and smoke.
I'd be too daughter of a son for them.
Sunlight reflects off a flagpole
like the gleam of a black cherry.
A wildfire, controlled, burns
in the rearview. Every city
has a graveyard; this will not
be mine.

PART FOUR

The Garden of My Memory

PEOPLE YOUNGER THAN ME ARE GETTING CANCER

ALISON STONE

Liver, stomach, lung—
The body preying on itself.
Limbs withering, bones lit with pain.
Still, the undimmed craving for more life.

Six vultures circle
a deer down in the field.
Does their wild hunger make us turn away?
There I go, talking about hunger again.
Maybe the reason for my obsession is simple—my slender,
obedient mother, told to gain
no more than ten pounds during pregnancy,
gained five.

The radio keeps blaring Yemen.
What the emaciated children weigh, how
they won't laugh. Each time,
I write a helpful check or don't,
then turn it off.

Teen years I pushed food away,
a self made by refusal.
In life's second half, I've morphed
to someone who devours,
knowing that every offer's finite.
I lift my face to the beginning
of a storm. Rain mackles
the zaftig moon. Above the wind,
a captured animal cries out.

BEYOND THE GRAVE

LAUREL BENJAMIN

162

The neurologist skooches over to display my brain on the computer screen. I say, *My mother's brain*, a whole hemisphere missing. Surely that would explain the nerve pain. He squeezes something out of a tube, places his thumbs behind my ears. I say, *This will hurt after.*

I only know a quarter of what he knows about nerve endings, don't close my eyes, stare at the brain scan, see an overlay that can't be explained—my mother's scan, not shown to us after her stroke but at the second hospital, like a watercolor. Has someone applied blush on the right hemisphere?

My cousin calls me, says, *Your mother was happy you didn't have children*, beyond the grave talk I don't need, because what did my mother really mean? Did she tell my cousin this, while squeezing toothpaste out of a tube, while washing dishes, while counting quarters for the pool locker, while on the phone?

My mother described to me her cat grandchildren as definitive, the same tone as my cousin who rambled. My mother was a warrior of driving down chance by planning so most things could be predicted in the wide plaid pants she wore.

The brain doctor doesn't hear me. Leans in as if I baked a cake and he wants a slice. Yet he doesn't notice my mother has entered the room or someone who looks like her is leaving a trail of ash over the exam room floor.

He can't perceive the cloak covering the shoulders of the woman, swimsuit peeking out, her face pasty with sunscreen. A good ghost. Goggles around her neck.

She is dripping wet all over the tiled floor.

Dripping wet all over my body while the doctor manipulates the space behind my ears, against my skull, infiltrating the nerve endings.

I remember when I brought my mother to her regular doctor after her stroke so he could check her medication because she would stand up and fall down. He came into the room, took one look. Changing her medication wouldn't fix her brain, half a hemisphere wiped out, brain playing a chess game, where a hand brushed the pieces off the table, out of the brain.

I hear my brain doctor say, *Your brain shows you've lived a healthy life.* I separate myself from the memory to hear him, separate from my mother-ghost in the room, from my mother's brain scan.

My fingers rip out the stiches stitching us together.

Wasn't I the hand that swept the chess pieces off the table? Wasn't it my fault for not calling her back the day of her stroke, out walking, tired of her not listening to me or her doctor?

I tell the neurologist, *The space behind my ears is where I hide things.*

FEVER: 104°

KATHY PAUL

And then I lost two days   But my mother, she fought:
it was so easy to slip   struggling within herself
into the nowhere   from her breath
no hands reached out   to her shell, until
across the divide   she rolled and clutched
and there were voices   fearfully, horribly the
blue ice packed against my naked cold metal railing
body so close so close   then I whispered
I don't remember   that we would be
falling don't remember   right there, would care for
oblivion and   her sister, would care
the second time—   for her cats—
I simply wasn't.   She opened her hands

And then I was again.   and she wasn't

THE PACT

ALISHA BLANCH

I made a deal with the dusk—
not the devil,
but something softer,
with hands made of candle smoke
and a voice like distant thunder.

I said: one more day.
Let me wake tomorrow
and I will write a poem
sharp enough to open
whatever cage I'm in.

It nodded.
No contracts,
no blood.
Just breath held long enough
to feel like prayer.

Some nights,
I forget I'm still here.
I walk through my body
like a stranger's house,
touching the walls gently,
as if memory might wake
and forgive me.

But every morning,
the deal holds.
I wake to sky.
To breath.
To birds who do not know
the weight they carry
when they sing.

And I keep my promise—
pen to page,
heart to sleeve,
writing toward the light
that does not promise to stay
but always returns.

DISCOVERY

KELLY MILLER

dig beneath the earth's skin
excavate the roots
of this grief
what do you find
in the biopsy of pain?
a tumor that feeds on
secrets we bury
skeletons too ugly
to dress for worship
sometimes there's no map
no destination
just a gravedigger and her pen
out searching in the moonlight
for any sign
of life

HIDDEN IN LIGHT

GEOFFREY HEPTONSTALL

The tenderness of the hour
when night is truly timeless
because the darkness dares not
say when morning will come.
Better to trust in candlelight,
the time-honored guide for travelers
through the inconstant sleeper's dream
when the shape ahead may be spirit
if not a working early riser,
a dawn wanderer in the borderland.
Some say that here is nowhere.
Who can determine when it appears
to be other than everywhere?
There is more truth hidden in light
than in deep darkness,
this rising revelation.

PORTALS

SUSANA GONZALES

This time of day when the house grows hushed
and the sun falls softer through the shades,
and evening is an actor waiting its entrance
in the wings, my memory slides backwards
and I feel Mom and Dad. Perhaps a portal
opens between the then and now. From day
to night the dusk allows a door for them
to step into this world. This world that's changed
so much since they last looked upon its face.
The earth that they once lived among is gone
and their child needs so desperately their grace,
their faith, their voiceless words of calm.
Death is nothing more than separate rooms
with doors through which we trade our love for love.

BISECTION METHOD

ANNE RAMALLO

The Will: Molly

"To my daughters, I leave my life's work.

"Do you remember the first time you held a snail? Maybe we found it on one of our walks after the rain, Lesma—leaving its glistening silver trails over a pungent sidewalk. Or maybe searching through the bushes for flowers to make your perfume, Zoa. Do you remember the way its body would bend, its long foot curling over the chubby contours of your palm? We'd watch it stretch its eyes out on stalks that grew and unfurled—past the point we thought there could be anything left! Almost like love. I want you to remember that.

"Out of all the creatures I've studied, I've learned the most from snails. Did you know that each makes two kinds of slime? The first helps it glide over challenging terrain, to climb walls or hang upside down. The second kind of slime, it produces in distress—to protect its delicate skin and help it heal.

"For years I have researched how to extract and concentrate these compounds. This is what I pass on to you. For Lesma, the power of motion. Take this compound and be impervious to the sharp rocks in your path. For Zoa, the power of healing. This jar will repair your wounds and help you regenerate.

"I can imagine your faces now. Lesma, you're grossed out. I see your nose wrinkle, your upper lip curl into a sneer. You roll your eyes. Zoa, your eyes are wide. The shock of it, the burden of sudden responsibility..."

The ache in my throat overwhelms my voice. I shut off the recorder and rest my head on the cool wood desk. There is so much to fix! My temples ache thinking about it.

I excel at splitting things apart—bisection. Cutting into my first snail at University, my hand shaking as my scalpel sunk into the slime and moved without resistance, I was sad to destroy something so beautiful. But that one act of destruction revealed ten new things to love: the pulsing glands, the winding ducts.

Bisection is a familiar pattern in my life now—the predictable pain of an incision that opens new worlds of joy. I split my career and my family life. After I had two daughters, I split my own heart in half. I could not have predicted the pain.

Two large mason jars sit on my desk, one nearly phosphorescent, thick and viscous, the other light and foamy like the edge of an ocean where it meets the shore. My culminating discovery. My final bisection. Soon it will be all that's left of me. I don't know if it will be enough.

The Letter: Lesma

Of course Mom was crazy, but I had no doubt her snail-goo concoction would work. She was meticulous like that. It was a big part of her crazy. So I had the power to move and stick. Only, I didn't know where I wanted to go. Just away.

A few weeks after her funeral, I gritted my teeth and put a dab of this stuff on my forehead, then I powered through my personal essay. I was able to address college applications with logical detachment, just like Mom would have. And it must have been pretty good, because I got in everywhere, and faster than I could process, I was far away.

Off in college, I asked myself what I would do if I didn't have to worry about roadblocks. But I couldn't come up with a good answer. There was nothing I cared enough about to stick to, so I put some goo on my hands, passed my commercial license test, and got a job as a big rig trucker. How's that for motion?

It suited me. Do you ever see these big trucks get stuck around a tight corner and start this halting, back and forth dance to get around a light post? That was never me. I flowed like a nimble kayak down a river of traffic, glided over mountains and flat fields, jotting my thoughts down in notebooks at truck stops. I rubbed some of Mom's goo over my skin and was impervious to the cat calls of the other truckers, hunched over their cups of coffee. Is your battery dead? I'd love to jump you…

Then I met a hitchhiker. It was his sign that stopped me: A story for a ride? He did not disappoint. At one of our rest stops I let him read through my notebook and he loved it, and suddenly I loved it and I wanted to keep going and write a whole book just for him. For the first time in a long time, the world made sense.

My hand and my brain were good friends already—they knew how to cooperate and move a story along. Now my heart wanted in on the relationship. And it hurt. I felt physical pain when I sat down to write. I rubbed some goo over my chest, and my hand kept moving, but the pain only got worse. That's when I knew I had something good that I'd never be able to finish. Unless...

You know, Mom said a snail could crawl on a razor's edge and not be cut. But I can't move past a wound that's already part of me. Zoa, I'm sorry this is what it takes before I come to you. There's something living in me that needs to get out. For someone who's good at moving, I can't get out of my own way. You probably hate me, but please listen. It's important.

The Ache: Zoa

I healed myself after Mom died. It didn't feel right using her potion. What if I used it up? I was not even bleeding. But the ache that had settled in my throat made it hard to breathe. I thought about giving myself a tracheotomy. I held Mom's scalpel in front of the mirror. Its cold metal soothed my hand, and I wondered if it would be possible to relieve the pressure, let some air in.

On a whim I turned the blade and slid it across my finger. Now I was bleeding, a thin ribbon oozing from the incision on the pad of my index finger. I bit my lip against the sharp pain. It seemed like a good enough excuse to open the potion. I plunged my finger into the jar and brought it up dripping long strands of bubbling slime, a string of pearls. Immediately, the bleeding stopped and I felt relief. An absence. With my finger still trailing an excess of slime, I painted a snail trail over my throat, feeling the outline of my larynx and trachea. I felt the absence spread to displace the choking knots. My lungs pulled in air like something starved. Once I was able to breathe, I could cry.

I tried the potion again after Lesma left, but it didn't work in the same way. When her car disappeared around the corner, on its way across the country, my ears ached from the silence in our house. I used to complain about the sound of Lesma's voice, always playing at high volume. No one could hear me over her

her incessant flow. Now I was so full of absence that the potion didn't provide much relief. I was missing another half. A wound can only heal if the severed flesh is there to re-join; otherwise the body just adapts. I adapted.

That was the last time I used the potion on myself. I used some on the cat once, when she came home with a gaping abscess in her chin. And on Dad a few times, after his knees started bothering him. Dad said I should go to medical school, but the closest one was three hours away. I couldn't bear to sever that last tie with Dad and home. I took nursing classes at the community college.

I was used to my life the way it was. I would say I'd healed…until Lesma's letter ripped me wide open again. A few days later she pulled up in a noisy eighteen-wheeler that took up the entire curb in front of the house. Typical.

This time was different, though. I had something she wanted. I could tell by the way she lingered in the cab instead of waltzing in like she owned the place. She didn't own anything here anymore. I had donated all her clothes and books after she didn't come back from college.

I watched Lesma throughout the day, observing what unimpeded motion does to someone, what Mom had done for her. She moved more slowly now, without the reckless energy that drove her when she'd jump on top of a tower I'd built or charm my friends with her effortless magnetism. She was more subdued now, and somehow even more confident. I wondered how she saw me.

"You look good," Lesma said to me that night after Dad had gone to bed. She paused. "How did you do it? What was it like?"

"Absence."

Lesma grimaced, her nose wrinkling at the bridge. "That sounds terrible."

"No," I corrected. "Pain is the body's signal to run away. Without it, I could stay and rest and heal."

I had known what I would do as soon as I got her letter. I didn't want to then. She had her inheritance. Now she was coming for mine. Still, I couldn't deny her. Looking at her now, her body curled on the corner of the sofa, hands playing nervously with the pillow tassel, I didn't resent her.

I went to my room and retrieved my jar. "Where does it hurt?"

Lesma raised her hand slowly to her chest and rubbed a wide circle.

I scooped a blob of potion in two fingers and applied it to the spot over her heart, then we waited. "What do you feel?"

"You're right," she said. "It's absence. But not loss. More like a friendly silence." Tears quivered in her eyes and spilled over in glistening trails down her cheeks. Instinctively, I reached out to touch them. "Do you feel it?" she asked.

What I felt was wholeness, the missing part of me regenerating. I nodded, dislodging my own stream of tears.

Lesma, with all of her old energy, threw herself into my arms, her wet cheek against mine, and our tears merged into a single trail. I wondered why Mom had severed our paths, why she'd bothered to separate the two slime compounds. Why not one? It felt so good to be one.

"Thank you," Lesma whispered, her breath hot on my cheek. "You have such a gift."

She leaped up and ran down the hallway, then returned with a tall mason jar. Phosphorescent slime filled its bottom quarter. "You take it." She thrust the jar toward me. "You could go to medical school."

The knowledge came gliding in slowly. Finally, I understood Mom. If Lesma and I both had everything, we wouldn't need each other.

I reached out and grasped the cool glass.

MY HOMETOWN CEMETERY ON MOTHER'S DAY

SUSANA GONZALES

is like Walmart on Christmas Eve,
cars parked sideways, children hopping tombstones,
rival boom boxes praising God or Vicente Fernandez,
tunes most requested by the deceased.

The mourners bring beer and flowers,
balloons, food buckets, beach chairs, blankets and babies,
oversized umbrellas, and white party tents
under which sit those who gaze at the grass
and wonder how they have managed
without mama.

Though I sit apart from the revelers
we are siblings in the way we speak
the same language of longing.
Our first word   *mama*.

In my town Mother's Day is a picnic,
a long love letter until the lowering sun
says it's time to pack up the blankets,
say our good-byes, head back to the house.

Later the dusk will fall on the wide empty lawn
filled now with folded flowers, limp balloons,
and all those wanting prayers we motherless children left behind.

CAIRN

CAROL DORF

—*after Louise Glück*

When I put a stone on the grave
it shocks me the way grief flows
past all the dry creeks and leaves me
looking to create a meaning
that could be piling up
the way duff implies waste
which the dead leave behind
the dead who won't answer my questions
or respond to any of the signs I leave for them
rose petals and beer
suggestions of a life
far from the things that mark beauty
after we stop depending
on other people's sketchbooks
and then they disappear
the dead that is.

I WENT TO MY FATHER'S GRAVE TO ASK HIS ADVICE

LEAH CASS

But he wasn't there

He was in the phonons
Of fire whistles
And tornado sirens blaring

He was in the granules
Of my mashed potatoes at
The Thanksgiving table

He filled the alveoli
In my lungs when I breathed
Now, broken

Silent
Tasteless
Breathless

Words whistled
In the wind through
The arms of an
Empty chair

OBIT

DANIEL P. STOKES

Three years have gone by and things I suppose
    Are the way you'd suppose things would be—
Your flesh decomposed and your bank account closed
    And your memory depending on me.

GHOST SONNET

JEANNE WAGNER

My grandmother used to tell me how ghosts came into the garden at
night. She could trace their footsteps the next morning in the soft
soil beneath the windowsills, the indentation of their soles smooth
as filed-off fingerprints. They were the ghosts of her childhood
farm, who opened the gates and let out the cows from the pasture.
Those spirits were pranksters, poachers, saboteurs of boundaries.
They foiled the confines of flesh, each cell a small, insecure paddock,
a fortification that fails. *Why does the body try to hold everything
at bay?* the ghosts would ask, their voices plaintive, sibilant as rain,
unpunctuated, shunning the hard consonants; a sound somewhere
between a sough and a soft whistle without the shrillness of bone.
Not music, not melody, I understood that, but a language that
was absolutely pure, if empty: their windpipes made only of wind.
They'd sniff at our fences for pheromones, stroke the walls like skin.

NOTHING TOGETHER ALL AT ONCE

JOSH STONE

on the way home
fog so thick
like a swarm of bees
like a shadow forest burning
gray smoke swirling
we roll windows down,
marveling at the cloud we are in
cutting thick slices with our hands
this car, now a ship,
sailing murky, uncharted waters
street turned fleet
headlamps and taillights
anchors at stoplights
that's when, squinting,
we caught a glimpse
of something or
some thing or
someone
a specter
drifting or floating or
maybe
yes maybe
we saw nothing, together, all at once
yes. probably that, I think
fog
why did this cloud
on this night
on this street
at this light
decide not to float up

where it belongs?
then, we wouldn't have seen what we saw
that is to say, we could have seen,
there was no apparition at all.
my god

ridiculous
I don't believe in ghosts
except maybe at night
in the car
in the fog

INSTRUCTIONS FOR HOLDING A GHOST

ELIZABETH HOOVER

Never look her in the eyes
so she doesn't see the fog that she's become.
If she comes close with a sobbing moan
hold her
gentle
between the ribs so that only you
can hear her whispered longings.
If you offer her tea
she will stir it
slowly
waiting for answers you'll never receive
from the infinite ponderings demanded of the sky.
You need not question how she got here.
You already know.
The invitation was clawed from the travertine,
and enveloped in purple velvet.
Let her braid your hair in the dark.
Let her hum
like the wind that forgets your name.
She means no harm
and she will stay longer
if you make room in the linen drawer.
When she weeps,
catch the silken gossamer drops
in the palms of your hands
so you too can examine the depths
of the living dead.

But do not drink them.
they were not made for the stomachs
of those who are still tethered
by breath.

When she leaves—
and she *will* leave—
let the door creak.
Let the floor remember her weight.
Never say goodbye.
Just fold her shadow
back into your chest
where all familiar aches go
to feel wanted again.

LUNCH HOUR

AJ POWELL

12:30. Latte cherry blossoms on my tongue. Cacophony
of ice in the cup. Hunger barks from the recesses of a deserted-island stomach.
I'm two hours away in both directions from each brother. I know (as I'm sure
you did) how to be a useful little sibling: I scrub out older brother nosebleeds
and vomit from the bathroom floor. It's a methodical, knuckle-aching bliss that
reminds me this is the closest I can get to someone.
Later on: my small problems are heavy enough to crack collarbones.
I eat, I wonder if mom and dad's pseudo-chapel will save me.
(How many inside jokes before this is written in a foreign tongue?)
Nobody seems lonely here. Boys shout to each other. The sunglow tells
the trees to shed their nakedness. The sky is extraordinary blank and blue and
looks poised to swallow me whole. My sandwich is fine.
On the first wedding anniversary, they pulled me out of school so we could
traipse along the boardwalk. The music was loud. We didn't talk.
It was too nice to stay inside.

WHISPERS IN THE FOREST

MAKENA METZ

I want to burrow into you like the dead
need winter. Grave stones crisp with frost

and silence. I want to rake my hands through
your bones, kissing the marrow

at your center. I need to grow through
your ribcage like moss pointing north,

opening your skin from the inside out.
When I curl in darkness, I will plant a tooth

in your soil, hoping that when it blooms,
the point will draw blood.

TRIGGER MOVEMENT

STELLA STOCKER

I have never touched a gun. But I've watched my
father face a firing squad, each soldier a neighbor
recruited from their own wars, mostly against mold
crawling from under their vinyl siding and dying as
green stains in the sunlight. They spat bullets silently
at the sidewalk, like curse words when toddlers
creep too close to adult conversations. I clothed the bullets
myself in steel jackets, scarred them with every anger
and disappointing pep talk my father gave. The days
he reminded me *every good writer is depressed*
I lined up my industrious little poems, dressed in
institutional gray, and carried coffins down the line.

I drag myself to the graveyard he raised me in. His
mother slumps over an etched-stone easy chair. The
happy art she asked my father to paint is strewn in petals
of yellow canvas, the flowers crooked and leaning towards
shadow. But flowers are cliche. Sadness isn't, and pieces
of him are easier to understand. I find a telephone cord and
toss it over my left shoulder. I stay on the line with my father
as he phones his mother about bad luck, sick brains, and
parents that never loved right, even under threat of friendly
fire. I lean back in long grasses, picking blossoms off a
triggerplant, wondering who needs to die first to cull the sicker
from the sick.

SUICIDE TREE ON SONORA

MAY GARNER

I was eight when I learned
that grief hums.
Not like a song,
but like a ceiling fan
in a room nobody visits.
I left the backdoor cracked
for years, just in case.
Just in case you wandered back
to the scent of your own ghost.
Mother washed the blood from her eyes
with rose-colored soap,
whispering *we'll be okay*.
But her smile spilled sideways
and slept away for months.
Sometimes I think I saw you
in the backyard, where your tree stands hollow,
just like your memory.
Where the branch you hung your heave no longer grows
and the rope no longer swings.
Maybe I just wanted something to forgive.

VISITATION

TINA PARKER

The ghost of my dad came to me once
He was worn down as I've ever seen him
Bone tired haggard
Head in his hands sitting there in his
Wife beater when he looked up
His bloodshot eyes bore a hole
Straight through me as if to plead
Make it stop.

The ghost of his mama my fiery grandmama
Ruby walked right past me
She died when I was two and didn't recognize
Me all grown there in her bedroom
Just kept moving arms full of clean sheets
She was a worker and aimed to get the beds
Made up before supper.

Twice the ghost of an unknown woman accosted me
She was scariest of all and moved at lightning speed
Through the closed door to hover over my bed
Then a mid-air dart to-and-fro to-and-fro shook
Her head back-and-forth back-and-forth frantic
Till her long greasy hair covered her face so I couldn't tell
If she was me.

HE TOLD ME WHAT DOESN'T KILL ME MAKES ME STRONGER

LEAH CASS

So I sit on his grave sometimes
I open the apps
I read the headlines
I count the bodies
I shuffle the cards
I feel the future

I release the stories behind my clavicle
Screaming to be heard

I listen to my mother's voicemails
I think about her life
I breathe
I feel my body

I train my gut
To take a punch

HERE/NOT HERE

BRUCE MCRAE

My mother would often disappear
from this physical plane
without so much as a boo
or by-your-leave.

For seconds, hours, days,
her absence made a space in us
which would never be addressed
by God or Science.

In this unprecedented state,
my mother was neither dead nor alive—
or so we had to suppose,
her silence on the matter
as cumbersome as any monument.
A silence thickened with apprehension.
Silence, but with an edge to it.

Some things, they tell us,
should remain unknown.
We are mired in ignorance
and have given this value.
All is illusion.

And, yes, finally, one day
my mother left and never returned.
We placed a hole in the earth
and this represented our loss.
We carved her name into a stone
and this stood for human folly.

PRETENDING TO BE A TWIN

TINA BARRY

the poem swims beside
my mother, her untethered sister
in a rocking, saline sea.

The poem recites her stories,
embellishes moments she's proud
of, thinks of them as gifts.

The poem can tell you
who broke my mother's heart:
first Sheldon and last Eddie.

It remembers her
in the navy-dotted two-piece, sees the hat's swoop
of dark shadow across pale legs.

The poem forgets,
but like my mother's memories, the timeline
of history is fluid. It believes

there's no shame
in confusing the date of her birth
with her grandmother's.

The poem says, "I'm sanguine."
But I know better.

I'm further along
in this trudge
from then to now. Ready

to fold
the poem's hand in mine, to hurtle
past my mother's hobbled walk,
last tiny apartment, her children's
children, the red-faced wail of a baby,
the long train of wedding dress.

To slowly lift the veil.

THE LANGUAGE OF THE BULLET

CHRISTIAN CHASE GARNER

—after Kimberly Grey's "The Language of the Bomb"

I look back on my life now, how much
time I spent confined in a tight line of my kin,
single file like kindergarteners starving for lunch.
My primer ignites in a spark (so small it could have been
accidental), and I begin my whorl—quick, like an aperture.
While you shut your eyes for this half-second of necessary
transfer, I'm grateful for even the briefest existence. I admire
the gleam of the lamplight, the stew of stars, the wet drive
still rippling from slate skies, smoke sighing to heaven
from a thick, rust-colored drum of smoldering waste.
I enter, opening myself up in a dahlia's yawn,
then curl back until I am empty, nothing
but the sacred pulse of an iamb.

THE FLAME, IT FLICKERS

BRUCE MCRAE

Ten years in the all-be-gone
and your plot has narrowed.
The tiny raptures bud in May,
as they shall for ever after,
your perfect lawn indentured,
the path losing itself in evening,
that pine you'd planted fallen.

Ten years in your fraidy-hole
and the lords of the smallest things
still force their sway over the far-and-wide.
Your mother lives within your sister's memory,
your trials and comedies stunted,
the nights too cold, the winds too certain.

Bill, a kind of darkness covers our eyes.
The hand of some rough angel
has touched us on the mouth,
so whatever we say or sing or tell
means as much as little or nothing.
There are no ghosts left in this house.
We are not wanted.

PEGS & LINKS

GLEN MARCHAND

Aside a zinnia, near a garter snake, sat petals. I clump grass, kneel
to pick a feather, time has wings—those salvaged years, to redeem
by insistence, to settle into mestizo: darkened passion, the holy
lands, a soul facing himself: demon auras, area sound, variant
depressions. I take courage, adrift in volume, to hear silence echo.
Another is wiser, prudent, dark talents & excellence. I remain
mortal, sold to it, alive in its debates, threshed as ultimate
challenge. I need to believe in us, to believe in goodness, to witness
balanced behaviors. I won't drop names—many had it, most
miserable in private, contributing to Zeitgeist. I sense details. I
paint maps. Eager it seems to locate what's inside. Many live silent
lives, reduced to Condition, tending to excellence.

THE GARDEN WHERE I LEFT YOU

ALISHA BLANCH

I buried you in the marrow of my memory,
beneath a sky stitched with dusk-blue threads,
where petals grew from every whispered name
I never dared to speak aloud.
You became the garden—
not the stone, not the soil,
but the bloom between
what was and what could never be again.
There, time unspools like silken rot.
The clock forgets how to tick
when sorrow sips at the stem of a lily,
drunk on longing and lilac ghosts.
Even the moon bows lower in that place.
She, too, has mourned a thousand lives,
watched stars blink out mid-sentence
and kept their secrets safe in orbit.
I still walk that place at dusk,
barefoot and bone-deep in ache,
each step a pact:

if I bleed gently,
will the dead write back?

Once, I believed grief was a thief—
all jagged teeth and final doors.
But now I see it as a seamstress,
patient and cruel,
weaving loss into lace.
There are things that only absence teaches:
how silence has a pulse,
how memory clings like ivy to bone,
how love does not end—
it molts.

And I am not what I was.
Not since the hour the world split quiet.
Now I am soil, and shadow,
and the echo of your laugh in the wind.
Grief is a soft apocalypse—
a bang, a bloom,
an unfolding of all I loved
until it no longer fits inside my chest.
But even the hollow has roots.
Even the silence grows something.
And in that blooming dark,
I am stitched new—
by thorns, by memory,
by the quiet promise that loss
is just another name for becoming.

TAURUS SKY

CHERRI CASEY DOUGLAS

Galaxies, shimmer
a tapestry of might
fireflies, flicker
luminous in flight
underneath
a Taurus sky
she sprinkles
magic light
where darkness
is beholden to
the majesty of night

DIGGING IN THE DARK

JOSH STONE

we take turns digging in the dark
and bury her by flashlight along
the wildflower fence
together, we cry, aching sobs as we pass through the little gate
with freezing, dirty hands
we put the tools for gardens and graves in the corner of the shop
the seeds are there too—waiting
this spring we'll scatter them right on top
our beloved kitty, Lilly will become lilies again

EVENING COFFEE IN THE CORPSE GARDEN

CODY DRACO

I wish I could bring you behind the scenes
of my big dreams being planted
in the backyard of your southern small town
where my hands are surprisingly steady
as I sip on an evening coffee in the corpse garden
plotting a thousand future ego deaths I will undertake
wearing vulnerabilities woven together into a superhero cape
I would tell you that I'm maintaining peace with my own mortality
but since birth we've been the last of a dying breed
feeling insignificant underneath the menacing Freemason monuments
and moved to gratitude beside the modest tributes cradled in the baby section
I can no longer tell which sips are caramel macchiato and which are hazelnut
I guess matters of life and death have a subtle way
of making us feel emotionally mixed up

BUOYANCY

ANNE RAMALLO

I touch the warm star within me
and tear my heart open to see
that the river
pouring out of my eyes
lifts everything up.
It runs deeper than you can drink.
But I am not sad,
only full.

WHY?

ALISON STONE

We wipe tears on our sleeve. The dead stay dead.
No matter how we grieve, the dead stay dead.

Do angels guard us? Are birds souls of those
we've lost? *Don't be naive. The dead stay dead.*

His brother, tanned, in swim trunks, reaches out.
Despite a dream's reprieve, the dead stay dead.

Naked, pre-apple, were we immortal?
Too easy to blame Eve. The dead stay dead

or else come back in bodies we won't know.
Based on what we perceive, the dead stay dead.

Robot surgeons, men on the moon. Even with
what science can achieve, the dead stay dead.

Moved by his song, Hades gave Orpheus
permission to retrieve the dead. *Stay dead,*

Eurydice wished as she walked. He turned.
In the sad myths we weave, the dead stay dead.

Is that her voice? His sneakers on the stairs?
Our dumb senses deceive. The dead stay dead.

How can some sky kingdom be paradise
if we can never leave? The dead stay dead,

though Stone sees her mother come back in her
daughter's face. Won't believe the dead stay dead.

THE BACK WAY FORWARD

KATIE BYRUM

Your crisis of faith comes in the kitchen
where you ask how I keep going
if this is it.

I tell you I think we remain, if anywhere, in pieces,
in tucked-away places,
and how we're remembered.
And anyhow,
time turns its own tiny, endless deaths:
the you and I catching crawdads in bare feet
are as gone as anyone we've buried,
we held no funeral for the barn cat
who simply never came back (but
maybe one day, in a back-porch sunbeam).

Later, you add a notch over soft baby hair,
pencil-scratching into semi-gloss paint,
and sometimes our mothers' laughter falls out of our mouths.

BIG NOTHING

AJ POWELL

For Christmas Mom gets me *The Stranger* and a promised trip to Portland, Oregon. Three simultaneous perfect hells means the devil is out for my lonely soul. Amelia has wildfire hair and a steadfast belief that she will put on the best production of *Les Mis* this town has ever seen, god help her, but Allison dislikes her for reasons she can't elaborate on. Griffin watches the new *Jackass* movie. There is no ghost to soothe to sleep. April passes, then May; I do SAT prep while the grief sinks its teeth into my shoulders. Mom's lax attitude regarding frozen pizza on vacation helps us cosplay normal people. Do-not-resuscitate order on his translucent body in reveries. I forget to get everyone birthday presents this year. Lee spins star-bright silk from pens; I would do anything to be her mulberry leaf. Allison is the commander of Colorado's double-black diamond; I can't master the bunny hill. I apologize for spilling the chips on the counter but I get yelled at anyway. Rachel knows my secret after I get asked about boys and my lips twist as if I've been force-fed warheads. Chloe gets the job and I get to volunteer. I get serious about playing video games as if the keyboard is a defibrillator, and the wires are his veins, and the correct tap-tapping of my fingers will have him breathing again. I swear on my sorry life that two Xanax will kill me; I writhe in bed as god's hands clutch my throat. I tell Ezra I'm watching *Futurama*, and then he asks about it again months later, and I'm shocked because I had never met anyone before who had paid such close attention to minuscule things. Leave the cats in the west and wash your hands of dander. The sign in the laundry room says: *You've analyzed, scrutinized, experimented, investigated, dissected, pondered, probed and finally discovered the one eternal truth*; I wonder what it is.

THE END

POSTLUDE

The Eternal Churn

DOES HEAVEN HAVE A P.O. BOX?

EMILY DANIEL

Grief flows over me
Like a current
A mighty stream
Today is the day of my
Very first book release
And I just wish
I could have mailed you
A copy

ACKNOWLEDGMENTS

Thank you to all of the contributors, and to all those that submitted, who lifted up this anthology in its earliest stages to where it's at now. This project was a huge undertaking, and we could not have done it without the many supporters, readers, and followers that huddled beside us in the darkness as we stumbled along.

Additionally, some parts of this book previously appeared in publications elsewhere in print and online, and we would like to credit those pieces here:

VERISIMILITUDE previously appeared in *Monterey Poetry Review* in September 2025.

CONSIDER THE SPORES previously appeared in *Presence Journal* in October 2025.

VACUUM previously appeared in Dana Gillan's poetry collection *Intimate Nuances* in August 2025.

WEARY previously appeared in Quillkeepers Press in 2025.

For more information on the editors, contributors, or Poets in the Pines, please visit www.poetsinthepines.com.

AUTHOR BIOGRAPHIES

Joanne Harris Allred

Joanne Harris Allred is the author of three poetry collections: *Particulate*, Bear Star Press, *The Evolutionary Purpose of Heartbreak*, Turning Point Press, and *Outside Paradise*, Word Poetry Press. A chapbook, *Whetstone*, won the Flume Press Chapbook Competition. She taught for many years in the English Department at California State University, Chico. She lives in northern California.

Kiersten Anderson

Kiersten Anderson is a poet and undergraduate student at Washington University in St. Louis. Her work explores themes of grief, memory, faith, and womanhood through vivid imagery and lyrical introspection. She draws inspiration from everyday rituals, ancestral echoes, and the silences we inherit. Kiersten's poetry seeks to honor what is lost and illuminate what remains.

Tina Barry

Tina Barry is the author of *I Tell Henrietta* (Aim Higher, Inc., 2024), *Beautiful Raft and Mall Flower* (Big Table Publishing). Her poetry and short fiction can be found in *Verse Daily, Rattle, ONE ART: a journal of poetry, SWWIM, Gyroscope, The Best Small Fictions* 2020 (spotlighted story) and 2016, and elsewhere. Tina's has five Pushcart Prize nominations, several Best of the Net and Best Microfiction nods. She teaches at The Poetry Barn and Writers.com.

Laurel Benjamin

Laurel Benjamin curates Ekphrastic Writers and is a reader for *Common Ground Review*. Publications: *Pirene's Fountain, Lily Poetry Review, Cider Press Review, Taos Journal of Poetry, Mom Egg Review, Gone Lawn, Nixes Mate*. She is a finalist for the Cider Press Book Award Prize and has received an

Honorable Mention for the Ruben RoseMemorial Poetry Competition. Her work has also been anthologized in *Gunpowder Press' Women in a Golden State* (2025), *The Nature of Our Times: Poems on America's Land, Waters, Wildlife, and Other Natural Wonders* (2025), Turning a Train of Thought Upside Down: An Anthology of Women's Poetry (2006). Her new collection, Flowers on a Train, is published by Sheila-Na-Gig Editions. Find her at: https://www.laurelbenjamin.com.

Alesa Bernat

Alesa Bernat is the author of *Everything Is Fine*, a self-published poetry collection about Bipolar Depression. Her poems have appeared or are forthcoming in print and online literary journals and magazines such as *Boreal Zine, Sad Girl Diaries, Black River Review,* and *North Star.* Bernat's poem "Elegy for Heartache Resurrected" received Honorable Mention in the Seneca Park Zoo's 2024 Nature Poetry Contest, "Water Into Words."

Alisha Blanch

Alisha is a writer and poet whose work explores themes of healing, identity, and the quiet resilience in everyday life. Whether through poetry collections like *The Lines We Live Between* or through the imaginative worlds unfolding in her multiple works in progress, Alisha creates spaces for readers to feel seen, understood and inspired.

Mary M. Brown

Mary M. Brown lives with her husband Bill in Anderson, Indiana. Her work appears on the Poetry Foundation and American Life in Poetry websites and recently in *Rockvale Review, Christian Century, Thimble, Journal,* and *New Poetry from the Midwest.* She was formerly poetry editor of Flying Island.

Katie Byrum

Hailing from Western Maryland, Katie Byrum's poetry often explores the landscapes of memory, finding meaning in passing moments and echoes of the past. Her confessional style touches on connection, desire, and a quiet understanding of mortality in everyday life. Published in *Sans Merci* (where she won Best Poetry) and *Sincere Dalliances*, she holds a BA in English Education from Shepherd University and an M.Ed. from Buena Vista University. She uses those degrees in her day-to-day life as a high school English teacher to argue with teenagers about whether Romeo is a "simp."

Cherri Casey Douglas

With a deep-rooted passion for writing and all things Egypt, particularly its ancient civilization, Cherri navigated her academic path through International Relations and Egyptology at the American University in Cairo, ultimately earning her degree in Near Eastern Studies and Arabic from the University of Massachusetts at Amherst. Now a seasoned screenwriter with over a dozen completed screenplays, many poems, and two novels, the author resides in South Florida with her infinitely patient and supportive husband, their amazing teenage son, and two little pound pups who dominate their humble home.

Eliza Cass

Eliza is a mom who loves baking, reading, and always finding new ways to learn. Most of her writing inspiration comes from the little things in everyday life. She surrounds herself with strong women and truly believes that her female friendships drive and inspire her to be her best self. Her favorite quote is "A little bit of whimsy now and then is relished by the wisest men," and she likes to incorporate that into her day to day life.

Leah Cass

Leah Cass is a writer, mental health advocate, and lover of all things spiritual. She currently resides in Pittsburgh, PA with her husband, daughter, and two spoiled cats. She graduated from Chatham University with a BA in Psychology and continued her education in clinical mental health counseling at Duquesne University. A strong believer in the power of story to build community and spark healing, Leah loves using her voice to help others open up about their own experiences with mental health and personal growth. She frequently speaks at events and workshops on topics such as mental health awareness, post traumatic growth, and self-care. You can find her on Instagram as @elleunchained.

Wendy Chappell

Wendy lives on the beautiful island of Epekwit in North Atlantic waters. Smitten by bees and lilacs and stars, she is obsessed with dying and death, particularly as these draw nearer her. She is not a poet, though she would very much like to be one.

Tinamarie Cox

Tinamarie Cox lives in Arizona with her husband, two children, and rescue felines. Her written and visual work has appeared in many online and print publications under various genres. She has two chapbooks with Bottlecap Press: *Self-Destruction in Small Doses*, and *A Collection of Morning Hours*. Her first full-length poetry collection, *Through a Sea Laced with Midnight Hues*, arrived in 2025 with Nymeria Publishing. Follow her on socials @tinamariethinkstoomuch and explore her work at tinamariethinkstoomuch.weebly.com.

Emily Daniel

Emily Daniel is a writer and artist with an illustrated poetry collection, children's bedtime storybook, and cozy mystery romance among her list of published works. A homeschooling mom and nature lover, she enjoys spending time outdoors with her kids, growing her own food, hosting community events, and tackling new creative projects—all with a chai in hand. She lives in Florida with her husband and two daughters.

R.M. Davenport

R. M. Davenport graduated from the University of Maine at Machias with a background in creative writing. She lives openly as a queer woman who is focused on tackling difficult conversations around trauma, poverty and mental illness through the arts. She has recently had work featured in issues of *DuFrank Lit, the San Antonio Review, Feels Blind Literary*, and *Rockvale Review*.

Carol Davis

Carol Davis is the author of *Below Zero, Because I Cannot Leave This Body, Between Storms,* and *Into the Arms of Pushkin: Poems of St. Petersburg*. Her poetry has been read on National Public Radio, the Library of Congress, and Radio Russia. Twice a Fulbright scholar in Russia, she also taught in Siberia and teaches in Los Angeles. Donna Sternberg and Dancers is using Davis' poetry in the recent piece, "Ancestors' Voices."

Kate Davis

Kate Davis is a graduate student at Appalachian State University currently pursuing a Master's in English Literary Studies. She is from Lexington, North Carolina, and finds inspiration in the red-dirt nature she grew up in. She writes poetry and short prose, and hopes to do so for a long time.

Carol Dorf

Carol Dorf has received fellowships from the Hawthornden Foundation, Zoeglossia, and the Napa Valley Writers' Conference, as well as "Best of the Net" and "Best Microfiction" nominations. Their writing appears on the Poetry Foundation website, in several chapbooks, and in journals that include "Pleiades," "About Place," "Cutthroat," "Braving the Body," "The Mom Egg," "American Stories," "Five South," "YesYesPoetry," and "Scientific American." Founding poetry editor of Talking Writing, they taught math and writing in Berkeley USD, as well as at museums and conferences.

Cody Draco

Cody Draco is an emerging poet and transplant to Bowling Green, Kentucky. His work carves through raw emotional terrain, wielding sharp societal critique, surreal imagery, and language bent to his will. Unflinching yet deeply human, his poetry pushes boundaries while distilling meaning from the void of 21st century existence in an intentional effort to code a new masculinity. He can be found on Instagram @codydraco and at codinganewmasculinity.com

Billy Easton

After working for 40 years in social justice organizing and dabbling in poetry, Billy Easton is mostly retired and is taking his poetry seriously. Billy's poems focus on a range of topics including self-reflection, sensations, nature, and justice (and injustice). He has written numerous opinion articles, which have been published in a wide variety of newspapers and journals including *The New York Times, The Nation,* and *The New York Daily News.* Billy and his wife moved to

Portugal in 2022 where they have found inspiration from the Carnation Revolution and love the people, the culture, the food, the varied landscape, and la calma.

Andrew Eckas

Andrew is a writer born and raised in Colorado who now resides in Philadelphia. His story "A Little Ancient Promise" will be his first published piece of fiction.

Haley Edwards

Haley Edwards is a Kentucky-based poet, MFA candidate, and grown-up junkyard child. Her work has previously won the Sarabande Flo Gault Poetry Prize, and she spends her time navigating life as a single mother, running a community garden exchange project, and moonlighting as an independent artist and illustrator.

Renee Fegan

Renee Fegan is a graduate of the University of Redlands where she majored in theatre and creative writing. She currently works as a high school theatre teacher. She loves spending her days writing, cuddling with her two dogs and two cats, and hanging out with her three amazing kids. She is thrilled to be a part of this wonderful endeavor.

Stacey Foiles

Stacey Foiles worked as a filmmaker for 30 years. After a personal tragedy in 2001 she started working as a special education teacher. Now retired, she has begun to write.

Linda Freudenberger

Linda Freudenberger began writing in 2017 after the sudden loss of her husband of 42 years. She had her first chapbook published in 2024 by finishing Line Press, *The Other Side of the Bed and Beyond*, and is currently enrolled in the MFA program at Eastern Kentucky University for Creative Writing.

Christian Chase Garner

Chase (he/him) is a writer and exceptionally amateur baker from the Arkansas River Valley. His work has appeared in *MAYDAY*, *Cleaver Magazine*, *3Elements Review*, *Blood Tree Literature*, *Stirring*, *Book of Matches*, and *Sleet Magazine*, among others.

May Garner

May Garner is a poet and author based out of Dayton, Ohio. She has been crafting and sharing her work online for over a decade. She is the author of two poetry collections, Withered Rising & Melancholic Muse. You can find more of her work on Instagram @crimson.hands

Dana Gillan

Dana Gillan is an award-winning artist, a published poet and author, small business owner, curator, gallery coordinator, art superintendent, artistic director, art teacher, dance teacher, choreographer, four-time grant recipient, community activist and volunteer with a degree in psychology, dance/movement therapy, and the dance/theater arts. In addition, Dana and her children are domestic violence survivors. From that journey came a passionate re-emergence from the ashes, ablaze with healing and gratitude into a second life. A chance to do everything possible with the power of the arts and creation and connection to pass the healing forward to the community. For more, please visit: www.creationwithdana.com

E. Laura Golberg

E. Laura Golberg's work has been nominated for Pushcart and Best of the Net Prizes. Her poems have appeared in *Rattle*, *Poet Lore*, *Laurel Review*, *Birmingham Poetry Review*, *Spillway*, and *RHINO*, among other places. She won first place in the DC Commission on the Arts Larry Neal Poetry Competition. Her chapbook, *The Terrible Man on the Plane and Other Poems about My Mother*, is available from Bottlecap Press.

MJ Golias

MJ Golias is a neurodivergent, Greek-American writer who received her MFA in poetry from the University of Memphis. She writes poems, which have been published in various journals, nonfiction, and romance. She has two romance short reads out, "Greek Snowball Surprise Cookies" (The Wild Rose Press) and "Opposites Do Attract." She loves all things books and dogs.

Susana Gonzales

Susana Gonzales's poetry explores her Mexican American roots and the lesbian feminist experience. She has been published in numerous literary anthologies and journals including *The Power of the Feminine I*, *Sheila Na Gig*, *Gyroscope Review*, *One Art*, *The Santa Fe Literary Review*, and *Mobius*.

Daniel Gonzalez

Daniel Gonzalez was born in Anaheim, California, and earned his MFA in Creative Writing from CSULB, where he served as the senior editor of Fiction for RipRap Journal. He has written an award-winning short film, "Matty Groves," and has published short fiction & poetry in *ANGLES*, *About Place Journal*, *The Ana*, *Allium*, and *Art of Nothing Press*. He enjoys playing with his dog and writing about mortality, and those small human moments which we all share.

Keegan Gormally

Keegan currently serves as Retention Intervention Coordinator for Chemeketa Community College in Salem, Oregon. He has worked in higher education for eight years and is originally from Fort Dodge, Iowa. Prior to working and living in Iowa, Keegan studied at the University of Iowa and received a BA in English, then received an MSE in Higher Education Administration from the University of Kansas. Keegan enjoys writing, reading, following a variety of sporting events, and lives with his wife, Alyssa, and cat, Crescent.

Randal Eldon Greene

Randal Eldon Greene is the author of Descriptions of Heaven (Harvard Square Editions), a poetic tale revolving around a linguist, a lake monster, and the looming shadow of death. His collection *Blabber, Chat, Shouting-*

Match: 50 Dialogue-Only Fictions was published in July 2025 by corona\samizdat. Links to all of his publications, interviews, and live podcast readings can be found on AuthorGreene.com

Joyce Hayden

Joyce is a former university writing professor. An advocate for underserved populations, Joyce has also led generative writing groups for battered women, teens at risk and survivors of abuse. She continues to facilitate online writing classes and has taught a weekly Ekphrastic writing class for over five years. Her work is published in Al Jazeera and many journals.

Geoffrey Heptonstall

Geoffrey Heptonstall's fifth collection of poetry, *What We Do Well,* was published by Cyberwit in 2024. A Whispering was published by Cyberwit June 2023. His first collection, *The Rites of Paradise*, received critical acclaim when first published in 2020. *Sappho's Moon and The Wicken Bird* followed. A novel, *Heaven's Invention*, was published by Black Wolf in 2016. *The Queen of Alsatia*, a novella, was published in Pennsylvania Literary Journal in 2023.

Mark Hernandez

Mark Hernandez is originally from Colorado. He earned his MFA in Poetry from Texas State University in 2021. He currently teaches composition, Creative Writing, literature, syntax, and Honors courses at Texas State University. He has recently taught a course called "Death Plot: Fiction, Memoirs, and Poems," where students explore themes of death through literature.

Lori Hetteen

Lori Hetteen writes poetry, and then, because she cannot leave well enough alone, often creates accompanying artwork. She loves the natural world, quirky stories, black coffee, and paying attention. Her work has appeared in *The Joyful Life* and *Cut+Paste Magazine*. She and her historian husband live in Minnesota and have four mostly grown children, two dogs, and a tarantula. You can find her work at lorihetteen.com and on Instagram @lorihetteen

Elizabeth Hoover

Elizabeth Hoover is a poet of haunted softness and sacred defiance. Her work dissects the emotional aftermath of survival, stitching grief, resilience, and reclamation into vivid, metaphor-rich verse. She writes like someone who's held both silence and fire in her hands and lived to turn them into art. Her poems often explore the architecture of memory, the ache of identity, and the quiet violence of becoming. Ellie believes healing isn't linear—and sometimes, the prettiest things bloom from the wreckage.

Danuta E. Kosk-Kosicka

Danuta E. Kosk-Kosicka is the author of two chapbooks: *Oblige the Light* (CityLit Press, 2015), winner of the Clarinda Harriss Poetry Prize, and *Face Half-Illuminated* (Apprentice House, 2014). She is the translator for four books by the Polish poet Lidia Kosk. Published in P*oet Lore, Spillway, Tar River Poetry, Tupelo Quarterly,* and elsewhere. She serves as the Poetry Translations Editor for *Loch Raven Review.* Danuta grew up in Poland and now resides in Maryland, USA.

Özge Lena

Özge Lena is a worldwide published poet who appears in *The London Magazine, The International Times,* and numerous magazines across continents. Her ecological themed poetry earned Pushcart Prize and Best of the Net nominations and was shortlisted for Oxford Brookes and Plough Poetry Prize. Özge's poetry appears in many anthologies and was showcased at Barnes & Noble for Poetry Month.

Nathan Leslie

Nathan Leslie won the 2019 Washington Writers' Publishing House prize for fiction for his satirical collection of short stories, Hurry Up and Relax. He is also the series editor for *Best Small Fictions.* He is the author of thirteen books including *Invisible Hand, A Fly in the Ointment* (2023), *Sibs,* and *The Tall Tale of Tommy Twice.* He is also the author of a collection of poems, *Night Sweat.*

Abby Luby

Abby Luby lives in the Lower Hudson Valley. Her published short stories and poetry appear in *Parhelion, Persimmon Tree, Third Street Review* and *Syncopation Literary Journal.* Her poetry chapbook is being published by Finishing Line Press. As a journalist she has written for *The New York Daily News, SolveClimateNews, The Examiner News, The Recorder News.*

Lauren Madsen

Lauren Madsen lives with her husband and four kids in Utah. She loves photography, family history, dark chocolate, and spending time in the sunshine. Recently her poems have appeared in the *Vessels of Light* and *The Way Back to Ourselves* literary journals. While spiritual topics are often the focus of her poetry, she also enjoys eliciting a chuckle or two at her monthly poetry group gatherings.

Ronna Magy

Originally from Detroit, Ronna Magy now lives and writes in Los Angeles. Her recent poems have appeared in *Cholla Needles, Women in a Golden State, Sinister Wisdom, Rise Up Review,* and the *Los Angeles Press.* An alumna of Napa Valley Writer's Conference, she was recently honored by West Hollywood as a civil rights hero.

Glenn Marchand

Glenn Marchand is an African American poet-writer, concentrating on the human predicament and the existential conundrum humans are faced with, with an emphasis on the imposition of pain. Marchand has publications with *Academy of The Heart and Mind, Ginosko Literary Journal, Assisi: An Online Journal of Arts and Letters, Journal of Expressive Writing,* and others.

MARE

MARE is a poet, photographer, performance artist, yogi, and sometimes marketing professional who lives in Brooklyn, NY. Her work has been featured in the Jersey City Text-For-A-Poem project and *The Branches* journal. She is often found performing at the Free Form hosted by Third Space, reading with Poetry is a Team Sport, or teaching at Kula Yoga Project. She owes everything to the trees. Find her @mareinallcaps on Instagram.

Catherine McNiel

Catherine McNiel is an author, editor, and hospital chaplain. Catherine lives in Chicagoland with her husband, three kids, and an enormous garden. She's on the lookout for wisdom, beauty, and iced coffee.

Bruce McRae

Bruce McRae, a Canadian musician, is a multiple Pushcart nominee with poems published in hundreds of magazines such as Poetry, Rattle, and the North American Review. The winner of the 2020 Libretto prize and author of four poetry collections and seven chapbooks, his next book, Boxing In The Bone Orchard, is coming out in the Spring of 2025 via Frontenac House. Visit www.frontenachouse.com/product/boxing-in-the-bone-orchard/
for more.

Makena Metz

Makena Metz is a writer and songwriter for the page, screen, and stage. She has an MFA in Creative Writing and MA in English from Chapman University. Her prose and poetry have been published with The Literary Hatchet, The Clockhouse Review, For Page and Screen, The Fantastic Other, The Bitchin' Kitsch, Arkana, Strange Horizons, and many more. Find her work @makenametz on social media and check out makenametz.com

Beth Middleton

Beth Middleton is a poet and novelist living in South West England. Her poems are often inspired by the natural world, discussing topics such as motherhood, grief, and joy.

Kelly Miller

Kelly Miller is a poet, author, and mother who graduated summa cum laude with her BA in Creative Writing. Her poetry chapbook, *A Woman in Four Parts*, was published by Bottlecap Press in 2024. She is also the founder of Poets in the Pines, an emerging poetry collective and independent press, where she works as the co-editor and curator of their forthcoming anthologies, most recently *Made from Midnight: a requiem*. Her work has appeared in numerous anthologies, including *The Magic of Us* and *The Heart of Us*, and she was a semifinalist in Tulip Tree Publishing's 2024 "Wild Women Contest." She lives in upstate New York with her fiancé and four children, but still longs for the Texas dirt roads that raised her.

The curation of this anthology series and working with her co-editors Anne Ramallo and Leah Cass has been the honor of a lifetime.

Daniel Edward Moore

Daniel Edward Moore lives in Washington on Whidbey Island. His work is forthcoming in *Xavier Review, The Meadow Journal, The Stillwater Review, Clackamas Literary Review, Sagebrush Review, Gyroscope Review,* and *River and South Review.* His book, *Waxing the Dents,* is from Brick Road Poetry Press.

Dez Napoleon

Dez Napoleon is a poet out of Hartford, Connecticut—forged by heartbreak, healed by fire, and writing like her life depends on it. She doesn't do polite. She doesn't do easy. Every line she spits carries the weight of what tried to break her and the wild, stubborn love that kept her standing anyway. Desiree writes for the ones still clawing their way back to the light. She writes because silence never saved anybody.

Tina Parker

Tina Parker is the author of the poetry collections *Lock Her Up, Mother May I,* and *Another Offering.* Tina grew up in Bristol, Virginia. She is a long-time Kentucky resident and a juried member of the Women of Appalachia Project. Follow her on Instagram @tetched_poet

Kathy Paul

Kathy Paul is a survivor of many things, including cancer and downsizing. Her work has appeared in *Pirene's Fountain, The Examined Life, Last Leaves, Intima: Journal of Narrative Medicine, The Ekphrastic Review, Rogue Agent,* and *Luna Luna.*

Millie Percival

Millie Percival is a poet from Scarborough, North Yorkshire who has undertaken higher education at Lancaster University studying English Literature and Creative Writing. Her poetry currently undertakes concepts such as memory, friendship, and illness. In doing this she often utilizes form to convey both traditional poetic forms and more contemporary forms to develop her work. Her previous poetry has been featured in *The York Literary Review 2025*, *SINK*, *Poetically Press*, and *The Ekphrastic Review*.

AJ Powell

AJ Powell (they/them) is a poet and artist. A native New Yorker, they reside in the Hudson Valley. They are studying for a master's in creative writing. This is their first published piece!

Anne Ramallo

Anne Ramallo, co-founder of Poets in the Pines, is a writer, editor, musical theater performer, and mom living in Los Angeles. She has a BA in creative writing from the University of Redlands. Her poetry has been published in *Persephone Literary Magazine*, *Tension Literary*, and *Coin Operated Press*, and her short stories have been awarded in competitions by Reedsy, the Royal City Literary Arts Society, and Uncharted Magazine. Her micro fiction "Propagation" placed third in the 2026 Pen Parentis Fellowship. Keep up with her on Instagram @AnneRamallo

Russell Reece

Russell Reece's poems, stories and essays have appeared in a variety of journals and anthologies, recently *The Walloon Writer's Review*, *Blueline and Gargoyle*. Russ has received fellowships in literature from The Delaware Division of the Arts and the Virginia Center for the Creative Arts. He has received Pushcart and Best of the Net nominations, awards from the Delaware Press Association, the Faulkner-Wisdom competition and others. Russ lives near Bethel, Delaware on the beautiful Broad Creek.

Eli Rooke

Eli Rooke (they/them) is a queer, trans poet living in Naarm/Melbourne, Australia. They first found a love for storytelling through text-based roleplaying and believe that the best stories are those made in collaboration. They are a creative with Come Close and Listen, producing folk-horror LARP events and have been published in swine magazine and #EnbyLife. Their writing burrows into the themes of grief, death and identity before resurfacing, gasping for air.

Elli Samuels

Elli Samuels is a poet whose work has been anthologized and published in numerous literary journals including *Maudlin House*, *Pif Magazine*, *Penn Journal of Arts and Sciences*, and *Tulsa Review*. A cookbook author, runner, and yogi, Samuels recently relocated to Little Rock, Arkansas. She is moved by the magic of deep friendships, the insane beauty of birdcalls and a finely-crafted Americano.

Kayla Sargeson

Kayla Sargeson is the author of the full-length collection *First Red* (Main Street Rag, 2016) and the chapbooks *Head on a Shelf*, *BLAZE*, and *Mini Love Gun*, all from Main Street Rag. Her poems appear or are forthcoming in *5 AM*, *Cimarron Review*, and *South Dakota Review*. With Lisa Alexander, she co-curates the *Laser Cat Reading Series*. Sargeson lives in Pittsburgh, where she teaches at Point Park University and the Community College of Allegheny County. From January-August 2022, she served as interim director of the Madwomen in the Attic writing workshops.

Moudi Sbeity

Moudi Sbeity is a Lebanese-American author, poet, and transpersonal psychotherapist. Born in Texas and raised in Lebanon, he moved to the United States at the age of eighteen as an evacuee following the 2006 July war. In Utah, Moudi founded and operated Laziz Kitchen, a Lebanese restaurant celebrated by the New York Times as "the future of queer dining." Moudi was also a named plaintiff in Kitchen v. Herbert, the landmark case that brought marriage equality to Utah and the 10th circuit states in 2014. A lifelong stutterer, Moudi is passionate about writing and poetry as practices in fluency and self-expression. Their first poetry collection, Want A World, and their memoir, Habibi Means Beloved, are set to be published in 2026. They now call the Rocky Mountains in Boulder, Colorado home.

Yvette Schnoeker-Shorb

Yvette Schnoeker-Shorb is the author of *Shapes That Stay* (Kelsay Books, 2021). Her poetry has appeared in the *New York Quarterly*, *The Midwest Quarterly*, *About Place Journal*, *Medical Literary Messenger*, *AJN: The American Journal of Nursing*, *Grey Matter: An Anthology of Contemporary Medical Poems*, and elsewhere. She holds an interdisciplinary MA and has served in various capacities as an educator, a researcher, and an editor.

Gail Schulte

Gail Schulte was raised in a large clan of autoworkers and book lovers in suburban Detroit. Volunteer and professional projects have taken her from the seaside village of Bagamoyo, Tanzania, to Shrewsbury in the United Kingdom. A graduate of Michigan State University and the Vermont College of Fine Arts, her poems have appeared in La Piccioletta Barca, Kingfisher, Sinister Wisdom: A Multicultural Lesbian Literary & Art Journal, and the Lavender Review.

Stella Stocker

Stella Stocker is a poet from Illinois who graduated from Bradley University and is pursuing an MFA in creative writing from Hollins University. Her work has appeared in Folio, Broadside, Violet Margin, Loomings Literary Journal, Laurel Moon, Periphery Journal, Furrow, The Foundationalist, and is forthcoming in Prairie Margins. When not writing, Stella enjoys reading and hiking.

Daniel P. Stokes

Daniel P. Stokes has published poetry widely in literary magazines in Ireland, Britain, the U.S.A, Canada and Asia, and has won several poetry prizes. He has written three stage plays which have been professionally produced in Dublin, London and at the Edinburgh Festival.

Josh Stone

Josh Stone is a poet, percussionist, and assistant principal from Owensboro,

Kentucky. He holds a BA in Education with an emphasis in English and an MA in School Administration from Western Kentucky University. Josh enjoys spending time on the marching band field, and hiking with his family. He is currently working on his first poetry manuscript. His poems have appeared or are forthcoming in the *Harrow House Journal, The Pensieve, Half and One*, and elsewhere. You can connect with Josh on Instagram & Bluesky @joshstonepoetry

Alison Stone

Alison Stone has published nine full-length collections and three chapbooks, most recently *Informed* (NYQ Books, 2024). She was awarded Poetry's Frederick Bock Prize, New York Quarterly's Madeline Sadin award, and The Lyric's Lyric Prize. A licensed psychotherapist, she is also a visual artist and the creator of The Stone Tarot.

J.M. Summers

J.M. Summers was born and still lives in South Wales. Previous publication credits include *Another Country* from Gomer Press and various magazines and anthologies. The former editor of a number of small press magazines, he is currently working on his first collection.

Sierra Taylor

Sierra Taylor is a mother and attorney from Salt Lake City, Utah. She specializes in wrangling her three young kids, as well as legal research and drafting. When she's not writing poetry or legal documents, she enjoys eating copious amounts of Indian food, hitting the ski slopes, traveling the world, or rocking out to '80s music. She can be found online on Instagram (@sisiwritesthings).

Tomi Ojo-Fakuade

Tomi Ojo-Fakuade writes from Ile-Ife, Nigeria. His works have appeared or are forthcoming in *Brittle Paper, Obindo Magazine, BRAWL Lit, Octofest Poetry Anthology* and elsewhere. He tweets @Tomi_loluwa

Laynie Tzena

Laynie Tzena is a writer, performer, and visual artist based in San Francisco. Selected publications: *Allegro, Ascent, Bayou, Event, The Lake, MacQueen's Quinterly,*

Rabbit, Sonora Review. She received an Avery Hopwood Award in Poetry, and has been featured at the Austin International Poetry Festival and on Michigan Public Radio.

J.N.V

J.N.V. is a West-Texas raised poet. He draws his inspiration from his experiences, indigenous roots, and his best friend, Morgan. He is formerly of the Austin Poetry Slam.

Jeanne Wagner

Jeanne Wagner is the author of four chapbooks and four full-length collections, most recently, *One Needful Song,* winner of the 2024 Catamaran Poetry Prize. Her work has appeared in *Alaska Review, Cincinnati Review, North American Review, Southern Review, Poetry Daily, Verse Daily,* and *Ted Kooser's American Life in Poetry.*

Terri Watrous Berry

Terri Watrous Berry is a septuagenarian who lives in Michigan with her luthier husband. She began to see her work published following her return to college at the age of forty, obtaining her degree the same year the youngest of her three children graduated high school. This year her poetry has been included by *Red Rose Thorns, Libretto, Ghost Lite Lit, Culture Cult,* and *Moss Piglet.*

Jennifer Weigand

Jennifer Weigand is a writer and medical speech-language pathologist. Her flash fiction was an honorable mention in Creation Magazine's *The Midnight Hour Anthology.* Jennifer is drafting a novel. When she's not spending time with family, working, or writing, she reads, hikes, and lifts heavy weights. Connect at jenniferweigandwriter.com

ABOUT US

Poets in the Pines partnered with The Dougy Center for this anthology, pledging 25% of every sale to help families, teens, and young children through devastating loss. To find out more about The Dougy Center, visit dougy.org

Want to create poetry that has an impact on the world?
Join the movement below.